'IS THERE anything distinctive
land of the five rivers? I believ

Male writers try to project a macho image or men —
macho with a touch of *naivete* simplicity a modified
version of the *nihang*. But even within this stereotype they
have plenty of variations. No such Punjabiness is visible in
the stories written by Punjabi women or by men writing
on feminine themes. They paint on a larger canvas and
are, oddly enough, less inhibited in expressing their
emotions. Fortunately the perennial theme so common in
stories in other Indian languages of a woman wronged,
ever tearful, is largely absent in Punjabi writing.

Although I have picked up the best known writers from
the Punjab, I am fully aware that a lot of good Punjabi
writers have come up in recent years to them I tender may
apologies.'

Khushwant Singh

KHUSHWANT SINGH, novelist, storywriter, historian, editor,
essayist and translator, is one of the best known
contemporary writers of the Indian subcontinent.

LAND of
FIVE RIVERS

STORIES BY THE BEST KNOWN WRITERS
FROM PUNJAB

SELECTED & TRANSLATED BY
KHUSHWANT SINGH

**Orient
Paperbacks**

DELHI | MUMBAI | HYDERABAD

For Manjushri Khaitan
'A joint dedication from my wife
and me for befriending us.'

www.orientpaperbacks.com

ISBN 13: 978-81-222-0107-9
ISBN 10: 81-222-0107-5

1st Published in Orient Paperbacks 2006
2nd Printing 2006

Land of Five Rivers

© Mala Dayal

Published by
Orient Paperbacks
(A division of Vision Books Pvt. Ltd.)
5A/8, Ansari Road, New Delhi-110 002

Printed in India at
Dot Security Press Pvt Ltd, New Delhi-110 028

Cover Printed at
Ravindra Printing Press, Delhi-110 006

Introduction

I have translated a large number of stories from Hindi, Urdu, and Punjabi into English. They were published in various Indian magazines largely *The Illustrated Weekly of India* during the nine years I edited the journal. Some were subsequently re-translated and published in Tamil, Telegu, Malayalam, Kannada, Marathi, Gujarati and Bengali. I am not sure what provoked me to make a special compilation of stories written by Punjabis. There was nothing exclusively Punjabi about their themes and they had written in three separate languages and scripts. I am still not sure why this collection should be branded Punjabi because not all the stories are about the Punjab and some of the authors like Abbas, though born in the State, did not live there nor could speak or understand Punjabi. However, there it is and there is nothing I can do about it now.

Is there anything distinctive about writers born in the land of the five rivers? I believe there is. Male writers try to project a macho image of men of their state — macho with a touch of *naivete* simplicity a modified version of the *nihang*. But even within this stereotype they have plenty of variations. Perhaps that is why my two all time favourites have been Khwaja Ahmed Abbas's Sardarji (named by me as *The Death of Sheikh Burhanuddin*) and Saadat Hasan Manto's *Toba Tek Singh* (translated by me as *Exchange of Lunatics*). Both plots are utterly contrived and yet manage to portray Punjabi character and the tragedy of partition which so cruelly divided Punjabi Mussalmans from their brethern, Punjabi Hindus and Sikhs. No other short story or novel has been able to do so in so short a space and with such poignancy.

No such Punjabiness is visible in the stories written by Punjabi women or by men writing on feminine themes. They paint on a larger canvas and are, oddly enough, less inhibited in expressing their emotions. Fortunately the perennial theme so common in stories in other Indian languages of a woman wronged, ever tearful and driven to suicide is largely absent in Punjabi writing. In this collection, I have introduced two new Punjabi women writers, Ajeet Caur and Usha Mahajan. Ajeet Caur has emerged as among the best of Punjabi writers writing with irony, wit and sarcasm, on a wide range of topics. I describe her as new only because it is in the last few years that I translated some of her stories. Usha Mahajan's name will be new to most readers. When she came into my life some years ago, she had not written anything. She was a harassed and frustrated housewife who wanted expression outside her home. I persuaded her to try her hand at writing, because I suspected she had it in her. Her Hindi stories translated by me were published in *The Illustrated Weekly of India*. Thereafter she has appeared in most prestigious Hindi journals and has had a collection of her stories published.

Although I have picked up the best known writers from the Punjab for this anthology, I am fully aware that a lot of good Punjabi writers have come up in recent years. They do not appear in this collection for the simple reason that I no longer have the time or the energy to translate their works. And translations sent to me seemed to be inadequate; to them I tender my apologies.

Khushwant Singh

Contents

LAND of FIVE RIVERS

exchange of lunatics

Saadat Hasan Manto

A couple of years or so after the Partition of the subcontinent, the governments of Pakistan and India felt that just as they had exchanged their hardened criminals, they should exchange their lunatics. In other words, Muslims in the lunatic asylums of India should be sent across to Pakistan; and mad Hindus and Sikhs in Pakistan asylums be handed over to India.

Whether or not this was a sane decision, we will never know. But people in knowledgeable circles say that there were many conferences at the highest level between bureaucrats of the two countries before the final agreement was signed and a date fixed for the exchange.

The news of the impending exchange created a novel situation in the Lahore lunatic asylum. A Muslim patient who was a regular reader of the *Zamindar* was asked by a friend, *'Maulvi* Sahib, what is this thing they call Pakistan?' After much thought he replied, 'It's a place in India where they manufacture razor blades.' A Sikh lunatic asked another, 'Sardarji, why are we being sent to India? We cannot speak their language.' The Sardarji smiled and replied 'I know the lingo of the Hindustanis.' He illustrated his linguistic prowess by reciting a doggerel.

'Hindustanis are full of shaitani
They strut about like bantam cocks.'

One morning a mad Mussulman yelled the slogan 'Pakistan *Zindabad*' with such vigour that he slipped on the floor and knocked himself senseless.

Some inmates of the asylum were not really insane. They were murderers whose relatives had been able to have them certified and thus saved from the hangman's noose. These people had vague notions of why India had been divided and what was Pakistan. But even they knew very little of the complete truth. The papers were not very informative and the guards were so stupid that it was difficult to make any sense of what they said. All one could gather from their talk was that there was a man of the name of Mohammed Ali Jinnah who was also known as the *Qaid-i-Azam*. And that this Mohammed Ali Jinnah alias *Qaid-i-Azam* had made a separate country for the Mussulmans which he called Pakistan.

No one knew where this Pakistan was or how far it extended. This was the chief reason why inmates who were not totally insane were in a worse dilemma than those utterly mad: they did not know whether they were in India or Pakistan. If they were in India, where exactly was Pakistan? And if they were in Pakistan how was it that the very same place had till recently been known as India?

A poor Muslim inmate got so baffled with the talk about India and Pakistan, Pakistan and India, that he got madder than before. One day while he was sweeping the floor he was suddenly overcome by an insane impulse. He threw away his broom and clambered up a tree. And for two hours he orated from the branch of this tree on Indo-Pakistan problems. When the guards tried to get him down, he climbed up still higher. When they threatened him he replied, 'I do not wish to live either in India or Pakistan; I want to stay where I am, on top of this tree.'

After a while the fit of lunacy abated and the man was persuaded to come down. As soon as he was on the ground he began to embrace his Hindu and Sikh friends and shed bitter tears. He was overcome by the thought that they would leave him and go away to India.

Another Muslim inmate had a Master of Science degree in radio-engineering and considered himself a cut above the others. He used to spend his days strolling in a secluded corner of the garden. Suddenly a change came over him. He took off all his clothes and handed them over to the head-constable. He resumed the peripatations without a stitch of clothing on his person.

And there was yet another lunatic, a fat Mussulman who had been a leader of the Muslim League in Chiniot. He was given to bathing fifteen to sixteen times during the day. He suddenly gave it up altogether.

The name of this fat Mussulman was Mohammed Ali. But one day he proclaimed from his cell that he was Mohammed Ali Jinnah. Not to be outdone, his cell-mate who was Sikh proclaimed himself to be Master Tara Singh. The two began to abuse each other. They were declared 'dangerous' and put in separate cages.

There was a young Hindu lawyer from Lahore. He was said to have become unhinged when his lady-love jilted him. When he heard that Amritsar had gone to India, he was very depressed: his sweetheart lived in Amritsar. Although the girl had spurned his affection, he did not forget her even in his lunacy. He spent his time cursing all leaders, Hindu as well as Muslim, because they had split India into two and made his beloved an Indian and him a Pakistani.

When the talk of exchanging lunatics was in the air, other inmates consoled the Hindu lawyer with the hope that he would soon be sent to India — the country where his sweetheart lived. But the lawyer refused to be reassured. He did not want to leave Lahore because he was convinced that he would not be able to set up legal practice in Amritsar.

There were a couple of Anglo-Indians in the European ward. They were very saddened to learn that the English had liberated India and returned home. They met secretly to deliberate on problems of their future status in the asylum: would the asylum continue to have a separate ward for Europeans? Would they be served breakfast as before? Would they be deprived of toast and be forced to eat *chappatis?*

Then there was a Sikh who had been in the asylum for fifteen years. And in the fifteen years he said little besides the following sentence: *'O, pardi, good good di, anekas di, bedhyana di, moong di dal of di lantern.'*

The Sikh never slept either at night or in the day. The warders said that they had not known him to blink his eyes in fifteen years. He did not as much as lie down. Only on rare occasions he leant against the wall to rest. His legs were swollen down to the ankles.

Whenever there was talk of India and Pakistan, or the exchange of lunatics, this Sikh would become very attentive. If anyone invited him to express his views, he would answer with great solemnity, *'O, pardi, good good di, anekas di, bedhyana di, moong di dal of the Pakistan government.'*

Some time later he changed the end of his litany from 'of the Pakistan Government' to 'of the Toba Tek Singh government'.

He began to question his fellow inmates whether the village of Toba Tek Singh was in India or Pakistan. No one knew the answer. Those who tried, got tied up in knots when explaining how Sialkot was at first in India and was now in Pakistan. How could one guarantee that a similar fate would not befall Lahore and from being Pakistani today it would not become Indian tomorrow? For that matter how could one be sure that the whole of India would not become a part of Pakistan? All said and done who could put his hand on his heart and say with conviction that there was no danger of both India and Pakistan vanishing from the face of the globe one day!

The Sikh had lost most of his long hair. Since he seldom took a bath, the hair of the head had matted and joined with his beard. This gave the Sikh a very fierce look. But he was a harmless fellow. In the fifteen years he had been in the asylum, he had never been known to argue or quarrel with anyone. All that the older inmates knew about him was that he owned land in village Toba Tek Singh and was a prosperous farmer. When he lost his mind, his relatives had brought him to the asylum in iron fetters. Once in the month, some relatives came to Lahore to find out how he was fairing. With the eruption of Indo-Pakistan troubles their visits had ceased.

The Sikh's name was Bishen Singh but everyone called him Toba Tek Singh. Bishen Singh had no concept of time — neither of days, nor weeks, nor of months. He had no idea how long he had been in the lunatic asylum. But when his relatives and friends came to see him, he knew that a month must have gone by. He would inform the head warder that 'Miss Interview' was due to visit him. He would wash himself with great care; he would soap his body and oil his long hair and beard before combing them. He would dress up before he went to meet his visitors. If they asked him any questions, he either remained silent or answered, 'O, *pardi, anekas di, bedhyana di, moong di dal of di lantern.*'

Bishen Singh had a daughter who had grown into a fullbosomed lass of fifteen. But he showed no comprehension

15

about his child. The girl wept bitterly whenever she met her father.

When talk of India and Pakistan came up, Bishen Singh began to question other lunatics about the location of Toba Tek Singh. No one could give him a satisfactory answer. His irritation mounted day by day. And now even 'Miss Interview' did not come to see him. There was a time when something had told him that his relatives were due. Now that inner voice had been silenced. And he was more anxious than ever to meet his relatives and find out whether Toba Tek Singh was in India or Pakistan. But no relatives came. Bishen Singh turned to other sources of information.

There was a lunatic in the asylum who believed he was God. Bishen Singh asked him whether Toba Tek Singh was in India or Pakistan. As was his wont God adopted a grave mien and replied, 'We have not yet issued our orders on the subject.'

Bishen Singh got the same answer many times. He pleaded with 'God' to issue instructions so that the matter could be settled once and for all. His pleadings were in vain; 'God' had many pressing matters awaiting 'His' orders. Bishen Singh's patience ran out and one day he let 'God' have a bit of his mind. *'O, pardi, good good di, anekas di, bedhyana di, moong di dal of wahi-i-guru ji ka khalsa and wahi-i-guru di fateh! Jo holey so nihal, sat sri akal!'*

This was meant to put 'God' in his place as God only of the Mussalmans. Surely if He had been God of the Sikhs; He would have heard the pleadings of a Sikh!

A few days before the day fixed for the exchange of lunatics, a Muslim from Toba Tek Singh came to visit Bishen Singh. This man had never been to the asylum before. When Bishen Singh saw him he turned away. The warders stopped him: 'He's come to see you; he's your friend, Fazal Din,' they said.

16

Bishen Singh gazed at Fazal Din and began to mumble. Fazal Din put his hand on Bishen Singh's shoulder. 'I have been intending to see you for the last many days but could never find the time. All your family have safely crossed over to India. I did the best I could for them. Your daughter, Roop Kaur...'

Fazal Din continued somewhat haltingly 'Yes... she too is well. She went along with the rest.'

Bishen Singh stood where he was without saying a word. Fazal Din started again. 'They asked me to keep in touch with you. I am told that you are to leave for India. Convey my *salaams* to brother Balbir Singh and to brother Wadhawa Singh...and also to sister Amrit Kaur... tell brother Balbir Singh that Fazal Din is well and happy. Both the grey buffaloes that they left behind have calved —one is a male, the other a female... the female died six days later. And if there is anything I can do for them, I am always willing. I have brought you a little sweet corn.'

Bishen Singh took the bag of sweet corn and handed it over to a warder. He asked Fazal Din, 'Where is Toba Tek Singh?'

Fazal Din looked somewhat puzzled and replied, 'Where could it be? It's in the same place where it always was.'

Bishen Singh asked again: 'In Pakistan or India?'

'No, not in India; it's in Pakistan,' replied Fazal Din.

Bishen Singh turned away mumbling *'O, pardi, good good di, anekas di, bedhyana di, moong di dal of the Pakistan and Hindustan of dur phittey moonh.'*

Arrangements for the exchange of lunatics were completed. Lists with names of lunatics of either side had been exchanged and information sent to people concerned. The date was fixed.

It was a bitterly cold morning. Bus loads of Sikh and Hindu lunatics left the Lahore asylum under heavy police escort. At the border at Wagah, the Superintendents of the two countries met and settled the details of the operation.

Getting lunatics out of the buses and handing over custody to officers of the other side proved to be a very difficult task. Some refused to come off the bus; those that came out were difficult to control; a few broke loose and had to be recaptured. Those that were naked had to be clothed. No sooner were the clothes put on them than they tore them off their bodies. Some came out with vile abuse, other began to sing at the top of their voices. Some squabbled; others cried or roared with laughter. They created such a racket that one could not hear a word. The female lunatics added to the noise. And all this in the bitterest of cold when people's teeth chattered like the scales of rattle snakes.

Most of the lunatics resisted the exchange because they could not understand why they were being uprooted from one place and flung into another. Those of a gloomier disposition were yelling slogans 'Long Live Pakistan' or 'Death to Pakistan.' Some lost their tempers and were prevented from coming to blows in the very nick of time.

At last came the turn of Bishen Singh. The Indian officer began to enter his name in the register. Bishen Singh asked him, 'Where is Toba Tek Singh? In India or Pakistan?'

'In Pakistan.'

That was all that Bishen Singh wanted to know. He turned and ran back to Pakistan. Pakistani soldiers apprehended him and tried to push him back towards India. Bishen Singh refused to budge. 'Toba Tek Singh is on this side.' He cried, and began to yell at the top of his voice, 'O, *pardi, good good di, anekas di, bedhyana di, moong di of Toba Tek Singh and Pakistan.'* They did their best to soothe him, to explain to him that Toba Tek Singh must have left for India; and that if any of that name was found in Pakistan he would be dispatched to India at once. Bishen Singh refused to be persuaded. They tried to use force. Bishen Singh planted himself on the dividing line and dug his swollen feet into the ground with such firmness that no one could move him.

They let him be. He was soft in the head. There was no point using force; he would come round of his own — yes. They left him standing where he was and resumed the exchange of other lunatics.

Shortly before sunrise, a weird cry rose from Bishen Singh's throat. The man who had spent all the nights and days of the last fifteen years standing on his feet, now sprawled on the ground, face down. The barbed wire fence on one side marked the territory of India; another fence marked the territory of Pakistan. In the No Man's Land between the two barbed-wire fences lay the body of Bishen Singh of village Toba Tek Singh.

Stench of kerosene

Amrita Pritam

O utside, a mare neighed. Guleri recognised the neighing and ran out of the house. The mare was from her parents, village. She put her head against its neck as if it were the door of her father's house.

Guleri's parents lived in Chamba. A few miles from her husband's village which was on high ground, the road curved and descended steeply down-hill. From this point one could see Chamba lying a long way away at one's feet. Whenever Guleri was homesick she would take her husband Manak and go up to this point. She would see the homes of Chamba twinkling in the sunlight and would come back with her heart aglow with pride.

Once every year, after the harvest had been gathered in, Guleri was allowed to spend a few days with her parents. They sent a man to Lakarmandi to bring her back to Chamba. Two of her friends too, who were also married to boys outside Chamba, came home at the same time of the year. The girls looked forward to this annual meeting, when they spent many hours everyday talking about their experiences, their joys and sorrows. They went about the streets together. Then there was the harvest festival. The girls would have new dresses made for occasion. They would have their *duppattas* dyed, starched and sprinkled with mica. They would buy glass bangles and silver ear-rings.

Guleri always counted the days to the harvest. When autumn breezes cleared the skies of the monsoon clouds she thought of little besides her home in Chamba. She went about her daily chores — fed the cattle, cooked food for her husband's parents and then sat back to work out how long it would be before someone would come for her from her parents' village.

And now, once again, it was time for her annual visit. She caressed the mare joyfully, greeted her father's servant, Natu, and made ready to leave next day.

Guleri did not have to put her excitement into words: the expression on her face was enough. Her husband, Manak, pulled at his *hookah* and closed his eyes. It seemed either as if he did not like the tobacco, or that he could not bear to face his wife.

'You will come to the fair at Chamba, won't you?' 'Come even if it is only for the day,' she pleaded.

Manak put aside his *chillum* but did not reply.

'Why don't you answer me?' asked Guleri in little temper. 'Shall I tell you something?'

'I know what you are going to say: "I only go to my parents once in the year!" Well, you have never been stopped before.'

'Then why do you want to stop me this time?' she demanded.

'Just this time,' pleaded Manak.

'Your mother has not said anything. Why do you stand in my way?' Guleri was childishly stubborn.

'My mother...' Manak did not finish his sentence.

On the long awaited morning, Guleri was ready long before dawn. She had no children and therefore no problem of either having to leave them with her husband's parents or taking them with her. Natu saddled the mare as she took leave of Manak's parents. They patted her head and blessed her.

'I will come with you for a part of the way,' said Manak.

Guleri was happy as they set out. Under her *duppatta* she hid Manak's flute.

After the village of Khajiar, the road descended steeply to Chamba. There Guleri took out the flute from beneath her *duppatta* and gave it to Manak. She took Manak's hand in hers and said, 'Come now, play your flute!' But Manak, lost in his thoughts paid no heed. 'Why don't you play your flute?' asked Guleri, coaxingly. Manak looked at her sadly. Then, putting the flute to his lips, he blew a strange anguished wail of sound.

'Guleri, do not go away,' he begged her. 'I ask you again, do not go this time.' He handed her back the flute, unable to continue.

'But why?' she asked. 'You come over on the day of the fair and we will return together. I promise you, I will not stay behind.'

Manak did not ask again.

They stopped by the roadside. Natu took the mare a few paces ahead to leave the couple alone. It crossed Manak's mind that it was this time of the year, seven years ago, that he and his friends had come on this very road to go to the harvest festival in Chamba. And it was at this fair that Manak had first seen Guleri and they had bartered their hearts to each other. Later, managing to meet alone, Manak remembered taking her hand and telling her, 'you are like unripe corn — full of milk.'

'Cattle go for unripe corn,' Guleri had replied, freeing her hand with a jerk. 'Human beings like it better roasted. If you want me, go and ask for my hand from my father.'

Amongst Manak's kinsmen it was customary to settle the bride-price before the wedding. Manak was nervous because he did not know the price Guleri's father would demand from him. But Guleri's father was prosperous and had lived in cities. He had sworn that he would not take money for his daughter, but would give her to a worthy young man of a good family. Manak, he had decided, answered these requirements and very soon after, Guleri and Manak were married. Deep in memories, Manak was roused by Guleri's hand on his shoulder.

'What are you dreaming of?' she teased him.

Manak did not answer. The mare neighed impatiently and Guleri thinking of the journey ahead of her, arose to leave. 'Do you know the bluebell wood a couple of miles from here?' she asked, 'It is said that anyone who goes through it becomes deaf.'

'Yes.'

'It seems to me as if you had passed through the bluebell wood; you do not hear anything that I say.'

'You are right, Guleri. I cannot hear anything that you are saying to me,' replied Manak with a deep sigh.

Both of them looked at each other. Neither understood the other's thoughts.

'I will go now. You had better return home. You have come a long way,' said Guleri gently.

'You have walked all this distance. Better get on the mare,' replied Manak.

'Here, take your flute.'

'You take it with you.'

'Will you come and play it on the day of the fair?' asked Guleri with a smile. The sun shone in her eyes. Manak turned his face away. Guleri perplexed, shrugged her shoulders and took the road to Chamba. Manak returned to his home.

Entering the house, he slumped listless, on his charpoy. 'You have been away a long time,' exclaimed his mother. 'Did you go all the way to Chamba?'

'Not all the way; only to the top of the hill,' Manak's voice was heavy.

'Why do you croak like an old woman?' asked his mother severely. 'Be a man.'

Manak wanted to retort, 'You are a woman; why don't you cry like one for a change!' But he remained silent.

Manak and Guleri had been married seven years, but she had never borne a child and Manak's mother had made a secret resolve: 'I will not let it go beyond the eighth year.'

This year, true to her decision, she had paid Rs. 500 to get him a second wife and now she had waited, as Manak knew, for the time when Guleri went to her parents to bring in the new bride.

Obedient to his mother and to custom, Manak's body responded to the new woman. But his heart was dead within him.

In the early hours of one morning he was smoking his *chillum* when an old friend happened to pass by. 'Ho Bhavani, where are you going so early in the morning?'

Bhavani stopped. He had a small bundle on his shoulder: 'Nowhere in particular,' he replied evasively.

'You must be on your way to some place or the other,' exclaimed Manak. 'What about a smoke?'

Bhavani sat down on his haunches and took the *chillum* from Manak's hands. 'I am going to Chamba for the fair,' he replied at last.

Bhavani's words pierced through Manak's heart like a needle.

'Is the fair today?'

'It is the same day every year,' replied Bhavani drily.

'Don't you remember, we were in the same party seven years ago?' Bhavani did not say any more but Manak was conscious of the other man's rebuke and he felt uneasy. Bhavani put down the *chillum* and picked up his bundle. His flute was sticking out of the bundle. Bidding Manak farewell, he walked away. Manak's eyes remained on the flute till Bhavani disappeared from view.

Next afternoon when Manak was in his fields he saw Bhavani coming back but deliberately he looked the other way. He did not want to talk to Bhavani or hear anything about the fair. But Bhavani came round the other side and sat down in front of Manak. His face was sad, lightless as a cinder.

'Guleri is dead,' said Bhavani in a flat voice.

'What?'

'When she heard of your second marriage, she soaked her clothes in kerosene and set fire to them.'

Manak, mute with pain, could only stare and feel his own life burning out.

The days went by Manak resumed his work in the fields and ate his meals when they were given to him. But he was like a man dead, his face quite blank, his eyes empty.

'I am not his spouse,' complained his second wife. 'I am just someone he happened to marry.'

But quite soon she was pregnant and Manak's mother was well pleased with her new daughter-in-law. She told Manak about his wife's condition, but he looked as if he did not understand, and his eyes were still empty.

His mother encouraged her daughter-in-law to bear with her husband's moods for a few days. As soon as the child was born and placed in his father's lap, she said, Manak would change.

A son was duly born to Manak's wife; and his mother, rejoicing, bathed the boy, dressed him in fine clothes and put him in Manak's lap. Manak stared at the new born baby in his lap. He stared a long time uncomprehending, his face as usual, expressionless. Then suddenly the blank eyes filled with horror, and Manak began to scream. 'Take him away!' he shrieked hysterically, 'Take him away! He stinks of kerosene.'

lajwanti

Rajinder Singh Bedi

'The leaves of Lajwanti* wither
with the touch of human hands.'

A Punjabi folk song

After the great holocaust when people had washed the blood
from their bodies they turned their attention to those whose
hearts had been torn by the Partition.

In every street and bylane they set up a rehabilitating
committee. In the beginning people worked with great
enthusiasm to rehabilitate refugees in work camps, on the land
and in homes. But there still remained the task of rehabilitating
abducted women, those that were recovered and brought back
home: and over this they ran into difficulties. The slogan of the
supporters was 'Rehabilitate them in your hearts.' It was
strongly opposed by people living in the vicinity of the temple
of Narain Bawa.

The campaign was started by the residents of Mulla
Shakoor. They set up a Rehabilitation of Hearts Committee. A
local lawyer was elected president. But the more important post
of secretary went to Babu Sunder Lal who got a majority of
eleven votes over his rival. It was the opinion of the old petition

---

* *Lajwanti* — the touch-me-not plant whose leaves fold up if touched.

writer and many other respectable citizens of the locality that no one would work more zealously than Sunder Lal, because amongst the women abducted during the riots, and not recovered, was Sunder Lal's wife, Lajwanti.

The Rehabilitation of Hearts Committee daily took out a procession through the streets in the early hours of the morning. They sang as they went along. Whenever his friends Rasalu and Neki Ram started singing 'the leaves of lajwanti wither with the touch of human hands,' Sunder Lal would fall silent. He would walk as if in a daze. Where in the name of God was Lajwanti? Was she thinking of him? Would she ever come back?...and his steps would falter on the even surface of the brick-paved road.

Sunder Lal had abandoned all hope of finding Lajwanti. He had made his loss a part of the general loss. He had drowned his personal sorrow by plunging into social service. Even so, whenever he raised his voice to join the chorus, he could not avoid thinking — 'How fragile is the human heart' ...exactly like the lajwanti...one only has to bring a finger close to it and its leaves curl up.

He had behaved very badly towards his Lajwanti; he had allowed himself to be irritated with everything she did — even with the way she stood up or sat down, the way she cooked and the way she served his food; he had thrashed her at every pretext.

His poor Lajo who was as slender as the cypress! Life in the open air and sunshine had tanned her skin and filled her with an animal vitality. She ran about the lanes in her village with the mercurial grace of dew drops on a leaf. Her slim figure was full of robust health. When he first saw her, Sunder Lal was a little dismayed. But when he saw that Lajwanti took in her stride every adversity including the chastisement he gave her, he increased the dose of thrashing. He was unaware of the limit of human endurance. And Lajwanti's reactions were of little help; even after the most violent beating all Sunder Lal had to do was to smile and the girl would break into giggles: 'If you beat me again, I'll never speak to you.'

Lajo forgot everything about the thrashing as soon as it was over; all men beat their wives. If they did not and let them have their way, women were the first to start talking... 'What kind of man is he! He can't manage a chit of a girl like her!'

They made songs of the beatings men gave their wives. Lajo herself sang a couplet which ran somewhat as follows:

'I will not marry a city lad
   city lads wear boots
And I have such a small bottom.'

Nevertheless the first time Lajo met a boy from the city she fell in love with him; this was Sunder Lal. He had come with the bridegroom's party at Lajwanti's sister's wedding. His eyes had fallen on Lajwanti and he had whispered in the bridegroom's ear, 'Your sister-in-law is quite a saucy morsel; your bride's likely to be a dainty dish old chap!' Lajo had overheard Sunder Lal. The words went to her head. She did not notice the enormous boots Sunder Lal was wearing; she also forgot that her behind was small.

Such were the thoughts that coursed round Sunder Lal's head when he went out singing in the morning procession. He would say to himself, 'If I got another chance, just one more chance, I would really rehabilitate her in my heart. I could set an example to the people and tell them — these poor women are not to blame, they were victimised by lecherous ravishers. A society which refuses to accept these helpless women is rotten beyond redemption and deserves to be liquidated.' He agitated for the rehabilitation of abducted women and for according them the respect due to a wife, mother, daughter and sister in any home. He exhorted the men never to remind these women of their past experiences because they had become as sensitive as the lajwanti and would, like the leaves of the plant, wither when a finger was pointed towards them.

In order to propagate the cause of Rehabilitation of Hearts, the Mulla Shakoor Committee organised morning processions. The early hours of the dawn were blissfully peaceful — no hubbub of people, no noise of traffic. Even street dogs, who had kept an all-night vigil, were fast asleep beside the *tandoors*. People who were roused from their slumbers by the singing would simply mutter, 'Oh, the dawn chorus' and go back to their dreams.

People listened to Babu Sunder Lal's exhortations sometimes with patience, sometimes with irritation. Women who had had no trouble in coming across from Pakistan were utterly complacent, like over-ripe cauliflowers. Their menfolk were indifferent and grumbled; their children treated the songs on rehabilitation like lullabys to make them sleep again.

Words which assail one's ears in the early hours of the dawn have a habit of going round in the head with insidious intent. Often a person who has not understood their meaning will find himself humming them while he is about his business.

When Miss Mridula Sarabhai arranged for the exchange of abducted women between India and Pakistan, some men of Mulla Shakoor expressed their readiness to take them back. Their relatives went to receive them in the market place. For sometime the abducted women and their menfolk faced each other in awkward silence. Then they swallowed their pride, took their women and re-built their domestic lives. Rasalu, Neki Ram and Sunder Lal joined the throng and encouraged the rehabilitators with slogans like 'Long Live Mahinder Singh... Long Live Sohan Lal.' They yelled till their throats were parched.

There were some people who refused to have anything to do with the abducted women who came back. 'Why couldn't they have killed themselves? Why didn't they take poison and preserve their virtue and their honour? Why didn't they jump into a well? They are cowards, they clung to life...'

Hundreds of thousands of women had in fact killed themselves rather than be dishonoured... how could the dead know what courage it needed to face the cold, hostile world of the living in a hard-hearted world in which husbands refused to acknowledge their wives. And some of these women would think sadly of their names and the joyful meanings they had... 'Suhagwanti... of marital bliss' — or they would turn to a younger brother and say 'Oi Bihari, my own little darling brother, when you were a baby I looked after you as if you were my own son.' And Bihari would want to slip away into a corner, but his feet would remain rooted to the ground and he would stare helplessly at his parents. The parents steeled their hearts and looked fearfully at Narain Bawa and Narain Bawa looked equally helplessly at heaven — the heaven that has no substance but is merely an optical illusion, a boundary line beyond which we cannot see!

Miss Sarabhai brought a truckload of Hindu women from Pakistan, to be exchanged with Muslim women abducted by Indians. Lajwanti was not amongst them. Sunder Lal watched with hope and expectancy till the last of the Hindu women had come down from the truck. And then with patient resignation plunged himself in the committees' activities. The committee redoubled its work and began taking out processions and singing both morning and evening, as well as organising meetings. The aged lawyer, Kalka Prasad, addressed the meetings in his wheezy, asthamatic voice (Rasalu kept a spitoon in readiness beside him). Strange noises came over the microphone when Kalka Prasad was speaking.

Neki Ram also said his few words. But whatever he said or quoted from the scriptures seemed to go against his point of view. Whenever the tide of battle seemed to be going against them, Babu Sunder Lal would rise and stem the retreat. He was never able to complete more than a couple of sentences. His throat went dry and tears streamed down his eyes. His heart was always too full for words and he had to sit down without making his speech. An embarrassed silence would descend on the audience. But the two sentences that Sunder Lal spoke came from the bottom of his anguished heart and had a greater impact than all the clever verbosity of the lawyer, Kalka Prasad. The men shed a few tears and lightened the burden on their hearts; and then they went home without a thought in their empty heads.

One day the Rehabilitation of Hearts Committee was out early in the afternoon. It trespassed into the area near the temple which was looked upon as the citadel of orthodox reaction. The faithful were seated on a cement platform under the *peepul* tree and were listening to a commentary on the *Ramayana*. By sheer coincidence Narain Bawa happened to be narrating the incident about Ram overhearing a washerman say to his errant wife: ' "I am not Sri Ram Chandra to take back a woman who has spent many years with another man" — and being overcome by the implied rebuke, Ram Chandra had ordered his own wife Sita, who was at the time far gone with child, to leave his palace.'

'Can one find a better example of the high standard of morality?' asked Narain Bawa of his audience. 'Such was the sense of equality in the Kingdom of Ram that even the remark of a poor washerman was given full consideration. This was true Ram *Rajya* — the Kingdom of God on earth.'

The procession had halted near the temple and had stopped to listen to the discourse. Sunder Lal heard the last sentence and spoke up: 'We do not want a Ram *Rajya* of this sort.'

'Be quiet! ...Who is this man?...Silence,' came the cries from the audience.

Sunder Lal clove his way through the crowd and said loudly, 'No one can stop me from speaking...'

Another volley of protests came from the crowd. 'Silence!... We will not let you say a word.' And someone shouted from a corner 'We'll kill you!'

Narain Bawa spoke gently, 'My dear Sunder Lal, you do not understand the sacred traditions of the *Vedas*.'

Sunder Lal was ready with his retort: 'I understand at least one thing: in Ram *Rajya* the voice of a washerman was heard, but the presentday protagonists of the same Ram *Rajya* cannot bear to hear the voice of Sunder Lal.'

The people who had threatened to beat up Sunder Lal were put to shame.

'Let him speak,' yelled Rasalu and Neki Ram. 'Silence! Let us hear him.'

And Sunder Lal began to speak: 'Sri Ram was our hero. But what kind of justice was this, that he accepted the word of a washerman and refused to take the word of so great a *maharani* as his wife!'

Narain Bawa answered 'Sita was his own wife; Sunder Lal, you have not realised that very important fact.'

'Bawa*ji*, there are many things in this world which are beyond my comprehension. I believe that the only true Ram *Rajya* is a state where a person neither does wrong to anyone nor suffers anyone to do him any wrong.'

Sunder Lal's words arrested everyone's attention. He continued his oration. 'Injustice to oneself is as great a wrong as inflicting it on others... even today Lord Ram has ejected Sita

from his home... only because she was compelled to live with her abductor, Ravana... what sin had Sita committed? Wasn't she the victim of a ruse and then of violence like our own mothers and sisters today? Was it a question of Sita's rightness and wrongness, or the wickedness of Ravana? Ravana had ten heads, the donkey has only one large one... today our innocent Sitas have been thrown out of their homes... Sita... Lajwanti.'
...Sunder Lal broke down and wept.

Rasalu and Neki Ram raised aloft their banners: school-children had cut out and pasted slogans on them. They yelled 'Long Live Sunder Lal Babu.' Somebody in the crowd shouted 'Long Live Sita — the queen of virtue.' And somebody else cried 'Sri Ram Chandra...'

Many voices shouted 'Silence.' Many people left the congregation and joined the procession. Narain Bawa's months of preaching was undone in a few moments. The lawyer, Kalka Prasad, and the petition writer, Hukam Singh, led the procession towards the great square... tapping a sort of victory tatoo with their decrepit walking sticks. Sunder Lal had not yet dried his tears. The processionists sang with great gusto.

'The leaves of lajwanti wither with the touch...'

The dawn had not yet greyed the eastern horizon when the song of the processionists assailed the ears of the residents of Mulla Shakoor. The widow in house 414 stretched her limbs and being still heavy with sleep went back to her dreams. Lal Chand who was from Sunder Lal's village came running. He stuck his arms out of his shawl and said breathlessly: 'Congratulations, Sunder Lal.' Sunder Lal prodded the embers in his *chillum* and asked. 'What for, Lal Chand?'

'I saw sister-in-law Lajo.'

The *chillum* fell from Sunder Lal's hands; the sweetened tobacco scattered on the floor. 'Where did you see her?' he asked, taking Lal Chand by the shoulder.

'On the border at Wagah.'

Sunder Lal let go of Lal Chand. 'It must have been someone else,' he said quickly and sat down on his haunches.

'No, brother Sunder Lal, it was sister-in-law Lajo,' repeated Lal Chand with reassurance. 'The same Lajo.'

'Could you recognise her?' asked Sunder Lal gathering bits of the tobacco and mashing them in his palm. He took Rasalu's *chillum* and continued; 'All right, tell me what are her distinguishing marks?'

'You are a strange one to think that I wouldn't recognise her! She has a tatoo mark on her chin, another on her right cheek and...'

'Yes, yes, yes,' exploded Sunder Lal and completed his wife's description: 'the third one is on her forehead.'

He sat up on his knees. He wanted to remove all doubts. He recalled the marks Lajwanti had had tatooed on her body as a child; they were like the green spots on the leaves of lajwanti, which disappear when the leaves curl up. His Lajwanti behaved exactly in the same way; whenever he pointed out her tatoo marks she used to curl up in embarrassment as if in a shell — almost as if she were stripped and her nakedness was being exposed. A strange longing as well as fear wracked Sunder Lal's body. He took Lal Chand by the arm and asked, 'How did Lajo get to the border?'

'There was an exchange of abducted women between India and Pakistan.'

'What happened?' Sunder Lal stood up suddenly and repeated impatiently. 'Tell me, what happened then?'

Rasalu rose from the charpoy and in his smoker's wheezy voice asked. 'Is it really true that sister-in-law Lajo is back?'

Lal Chand continued his story... 'At the border the Pakistanis returned sixteen of our women and took back sixteen of theirs... there was some argument... our chaps said that the women they were handing over were old or middle-aged... and of little use. A large crowd gathered and hot words were exchanged. Then one of their fellows got Lajo to stand up on top of the truck, snatched away her *duppatta* and spoke: 'Would you, describe her as an old woman? ...Take a good look at her... is there one amongst those you have given us who could measure up to her? And Lajo *bhabhi* was overcome with embarrassment and began hiding her tatto marks. The argument got very heated and both parties threatened to take back their 'goods'. I cried out 'Lajo! ...sister-in-law Lajo!'...There was a tumult... our police cracked down upon us.'

Lal Chand bared his elbow to show the mark of a *lathi* blow. Rasalu and Neki Ram remained silent. Sunder Lal stared vacantly into space.

Sunder Lal was getting ready to go to the border at Wagah when he heard of Lajo's return. He became nervous and could not make up his mind whether to go to meet her or wait for her at home. He wanted to run away; to spread out all the banners and placards he had carried, sit in their midst and cry to his heart's content. But, like other men, all he did was to proceed to the police station as if nothing untoward had happened. And suddenly he found Lajo standing in front of him. She looked scared and shook like a *peepul* leaf in the wind.

Sunder Lal looked up. His Lajwanti carried a *duppatta* worn by Muslim women; and she had wrapped it round her head in the Muslim style. Sunder Lal was also upset by the fact that Lajo looked healthier than before; her complexion was clearer and she had put on weight. He had sworn to say nothing to his wife but he could not understand why, if she was happy, had she come away? Had the government compelled her to come against her will?

There were many men at the police station. Some were refusing to take back their women. 'We will not take these sluts, leftover by the Muslims,' they said. Sunder Lal overcame his revulsion. He had thrown himself body and soul into this movement. And there were his colleagues Neki Ram, the old clerk, and the lawyer, Kalka Prasad, with their raucous voices yelling slogans over the microphone. Through this babel of speeches and slogans Sunder Lal and Lajo proceeded to their home. The scene of a thousand years ago was being repeated; Shri Ram Chandra and Sita returning to Ayodhya after their long exile. Some people were lighting lamps of joy to welcome them and at the same time repenting of their sins which had forced an innocent couple to suffer such hardship.

Sunder Lal continued to work with the Rehabilitation of Hearts Committee with the same zeal. He fulfilled his pledge in the spirit in which it was taken and even those who had suspected him to be an armchair theorist were converted to his point of view. But there were many who were angry with the turn of events. The widow in number 414 wasn't the only one to keep away from Lajwanti's house.

Sunder Lal had nothing but contempt for these people. The queen of his heart was back home; his once silent temple now resounded with laughter; he had installed a living idol in his innermost sanctum and sat outside the gate like a sentry. Sunder Lal did not call Lajo by her name; he addressed her as goddess — Devi. Lajo responded to the affection and began to open up, as her namesake unfurls its leaves. She was deliriously happy. She wanted to tell Sunder Lal of her experiences and by her tears wash away her sins. But Sunder Lal would not let her broach the subject. At night she would stare at his face. When she was caught doing so she could offer no explanation. And the tired Sunder Lal would fall asleep again.

Only on the first day of her return had Sunder Lal asked Lajwanti about her 'black days' — Who was he...? Lajwanti had lowered her eyes and replied 'Jumma.' Then she looked Sunder Lal full in the face as if she wanted to say something. But Sunder Lal had such a queer look in his eyes and started playing with her hair. Lajo dropped her eyes once more. Sunder Lal asked, 'Was he good to you?'

'Yes.'

'Didn't beat you, did he?'

Lajwanti leant back and rested her head on Sunder Lal's chest. 'No... he never said a thing to me. He did not beat me, but I was terrified of him. You beat me but I was never afraid of you... you won't beat me again, will you?'

Sunder Lal' s eyes brimmed with tears. In a voice full of remorse and shame he said 'No Devi... never... I shall never beat you again.'

'Goddess!' Lajo pondered over the word for a while and then began to sob. She wanted to tell him everything but Sunder Lal stopped her. 'Let's forget the past; you did not commit any sin. What is evil is the social system which refuses to give an honoured place to virtuous women like you. That doesn't harm you, it only harms the society.'

Lajwanti's secret remained locked in her breast. She looked at her own body which had, since the partition, become the body of a goddess. It no longer belonged to her. She was blissfully happy; but her happiness was tinged with disbelief and superstitious fear that it would not last.

Many days passed in this way. Suspicion took the place of joy: not because Sunder Lal had resumed ill-treating her, but because he was treating her too well. Lajo never expected him to be so considerate. She wanted him to be the same old Sunder Lal with whom she quarrelled over a carrot and who appeased her with a radish. Now there was no chance of a quarrel. Sunder Lal made her feel like something fragile, like glass which would splinter at the slightest touch. Lajo took to gazing at herself in the mirror. And in the end she could no longer recognise the Lajo she had known. She had been rehabilitated but not accepted. Sunder Lal did not want eyes to see her tears nor ears to hear her wailing.

...And still every morning Sunder Lal went out with the morning procession. Lajo, dragging her tired body to the window would hear the song whose words no one understood.

'The leaves of lajwanti wither with the touch of human hand.'

A hundred mile race

Balwant Gargi

In a low thatched mud-hut the peasants sat and discussed how they could get word to all the villages about their urgent meeting. They asked me what they should do. I could not help them.

Suddenly a low timid voice startled us. 'Please give me your message. I'll take it.' He was a tough looking young man of about twenty in a frazzled shirt and patched carrot-coloured shorts.

'To which village?' I asked.

'To all the villages,' he replied.

'All the villages! Do you know that the meeting is to be held tomorrow?'

'Yes, I know that,' he insisted. 'There are only ten or twelve of them...the distance cannot be more than sixty miles. I'll cover it within a few hours.'

Did he mean it? I looked at him. His thick lips were like furrows in a freshly-ploughed field, and above them spread the bluish down of a moustache which merged into a sprouting beard. He had a long neck, a thin belly like that of a leopard and big knees, round like bronze shields. On his bulging calves there was no hair, only the tattooed figures of two peacocks. His eyes were dull. How on earth could he cover sixty miles in a few hours? Was it that he did not understand what we said?

40

Inder Singh, an old peasant with a brown gnarled beard, rapped my shoulder with his metallic hand and said, 'It is Boota Singh... from Bhagoo village. Don't you know him? He can run a hundred miles at a stretch.'

'A hundred miles?'

'Yes. A hundred miles. When he runs he leaves the storm wind behind...'

'A hundred miles!' I was puzzled.

'Have you never heard the name of Boota Singh?' asked Inder Singh.

'Never.'

'Boota is the son of Rakho,' began Inder Singh. 'He comes from my village. Soon after he was bom, his mother put him in a basket in the field where she was harvesting and went on with her work. The family lived in one corner of the field under a tattered straw awning. Boota's father guarded the crops from jackals, pheasants, rabbits and other animals. One frosty night he died of pneumonia. Rakho lived in the field with her little son. She got a small hill dog from a gypsy family. Soon the little puppy grew into a full-mouthed dog. Along with him grew Boota. He would twist his tail and the dog would yelp and howl and romp about mischievously, playing with Boota like an elder brother.

'Boota's childhood was spent chasing camels, colts, jackals and squirrels. He would run after the rabbits jumping over hedges, his dog at his heels. He became so agile that he could chase a rabbit, catch it, let it go and catch it again. A rabbit can run four miles, a jackal about eight, a horse forty at the most and the fastest camel not more than fifty miles. But Boota can run a hundred...'

'How long does it take him to cover that distance?' I asked.

41

'Twelve hours. A horse can run faster than Boota no doubt, but it cannot run a hundred miles at a stretch.'

Inder Singh looked at me and said, 'If you doubt my word you can test it. Give him the papers and he will deliver them by tomorrow.' He turned to Boota and said, 'Boota, my son! Take these messages and deliver them to all the villages. Go, my lion.'

He handed Boota the letters, told him the names of the villages and gave him full instructions to deliver them to the proper persons.

The following day, the secretaries of the peasants' unions assembled at the appointed time for the meeting. I asked each one of them, individually, who had given them the message. Each one replied, 'Boota brought it.'

After the meeting was over, Kumar Sain, the lawyer, Jugal Kishore, the retired headmaster, Ajmer Singh, the judge, and a few others gathered around Boota and talked to him. We felt grieved that such a wonder was not known beyond his village.

'If Boota had a chance to go to London and run a cross-country race, he would make the name of the little village of Bhagoo shine on the map of the world,' declared the headmaster.

'Our country is full of wonders,' added Kumar Sain. 'We have great divers, wrestlers and hunters but they waste their talent and die unknown.'

'If Boota can run a hundred miles, no power on earth can stop him from attaining world fame,' concluded the judge.

An aged military *havaldar* said, 'His Highness the Maharaja of Patiala is very fond of games and sports. If somehow we can get this news to the ears of His Highness, he will surely send Boota to an international athletic tournament.'

A cunning, one-eyed petition-writer said, 'Has anyone tested Boota to see if he can run a hundred miles?'

42

A bald-headed shopkeeper looked doubtfully at Boota and remarked, 'A peasant's sense of distance is very vague. If a man runs as much as thirty miles, he believes he has run a hundred.'

'Why not arrange a race in our town,' suggested the headmaster.' The distance round the big common meadow is about 440 yards. If Boota completes four hundred rounds of this meadow, he will have run one hundred miles. All of us will watch and enjoy it. After this we can plan his future.' Everybody was thrilled by this proposal.

I asked Boota Singh if he would like to run around the meadow. He blinked his eyes and merely said, 'As you please.'

Maroo, the village drummer announced the news, 'Listen, everybody! On Sunday morning at seven o'clock Boota Singh, the famous runner, will run a hundred miles race. The people of the town are requested to visit the common meadow and watch this wonderful spectacle.' Dum! Dum! Dum!

Early on Sunday people gathered in the meadow to see Boota Singh. He was wearing dull, *khaddar* shorts and a flame-coloured kerchief tied round his long black hair which was rolled up on the top of his head into a big knot. At seven, the retired headmaster, who acted as the referee, whistled and Boota started his solitary race.

People continued to arrive till eight o'clock. The headmaster sat watching Boota going round and round the meadow with the same speed, in the same posture and with the same machine-like rhythm. The women came flouncing their skirts and sat at one side of the meadow, gossiping about village scandals, deaths and births and watching Boota going round and round.

At noon Boota stopped, drank a jug of milk which the drummer brought for him, changed his drenched shorts which were clinging to his body, combed his hair and twisted it into a ball on the top of his head, tied his kerchief around it and again

43

started running. He ran on till evening and finished four hundred rounds of the meadow by-six-thirty, half an hour before his scheduled time. The sun was setting. In its rays the wisps of Boota's hair, straggling from his flame-coloured kerchief, looked like glowing feathers. His chest heaved and over his bronze body perspiration streamed.

The crowd cheered him. Two people carried him on their shoulders to the *bazaar*. The news hummed through the village. Boota said, 'It is God's will. His strength runs in my bones. That's how I could run this hundred miles.'

We gave the news to a local paper and made plans to send him to Patiala for an interview with His Highness.

On the third day, Boota's mother came from the village. She was about sixty years old, a stout peasant woman with thick lips like her son's and small bleary eyes. She had come to take him back. We tried to convince her that a great future awaited Boota, but she would not listen to us. She said, 'I can't look after the farm. Who will drive away the jackals and rabbits from the crops? The old dog is dead. I am left with no one but my son. I can't live without him.'

'Old mother, your son is a world champion and you are holding him in a field under your skirt. His place is not in a remote village but in a city. The world must know about him. You are blocking his career. Don't be selfish and ignorant and foolish. Leave him with us,' we all implored.

She listened with distrust in her eyes and then repeated with a grunt, 'I can't live without my son. I must take him back with me.'

But when the judge said that an interview with His Highness was being arranged, she agreed.

'Don't worry, mother,' said Boota. 'Soon I shall go across the seven seas and run a hundred miles race in London and then the whole world will know me. Then we shall be rich and I shall come back to the village. Only I must have a chance to go to London.'

The following day she went back to the village, leaving her son.

He stayed with the retired judge at the outskirts of the town. The judge and his friends played bridge in the afternoon and Boota sat alone outside on the verandah, lost in his thoughts. We had sent two letters, one to the Officer of Sports in Patiala and the other to the Maharaja, and we awaited their replies. Early in the morning Boota would run with his long wild strides to the Post Office to bring mail to the judge. Sometimes in the afternoon he would race to the market and fetch betel leaves, cigarettes, ice or lemons for the people who played cards. The number of those who gathered at the judge's bungalow to see Boota dwindled. The aura of novelty about him disappeared. Three weeks passed. Boota felt as if months had rolled by.

One day he said to me, 'Sir, I know a man who was once in the court of the Maharaja of Patiala but now he is staying at Faridkot. He knows the Maharaja very well. If I go to him, he can easily introduce me. Then I can make my way.'

A week later Boota left for Faridkot.

After some time I heard that Boota had gone to Patiala. A long chain of references ultimately led him to the Maharaja's aide-de-camp, who promised to arrange an interview with His Highness.

Meanwhile the country was partitioned. I shifted to Delhi and lost touch with Boota.

It was sometime in the middle of 1948, the time of the integration of States into the Union. Sardar Patel, the Deputy Prime Minister, was touring the country, negotiating with the Princes.

I was in Patiala that day. There was a big procession. Sardar Patel and the Maharaja sat side-by-side in an open car. People in multi-coloured turbans lined the streets. In the crowd I caught a glimpse of Boota. He was watching the car move sedately behind the military band with its gleaming instruments and well-laced liveries.

I asked him what had happened to his interview. He said, 'Just now the Maharaja is busy with important affairs of State. When he is free, I shall have my interview.'

I returned to Delhi and did not see Boota for two years. But I kept hearing bits of news about him. He waited at Patiala for his interview. Each time some urgent State matter occupied the attention of the Maharaja. The aide-de-camp asked Boota if he would like to take a job in Patiala instead of going back and forth to his village, wasting time and money. At the first opportunity he would be granted an interview and be sent to the Olympics. This appealed to Boota and he become a watchman in the Royal kitchen. His pay was like a stipend. He had little to do but sit on a small stool, yawn and bask in the sun or roam about in the garden.

Once more his mother came to take him back to her village. But Boota, who had come to know the routine of life in the town, with its delays and red-tape, asked her to return, assuring her that all their troubles would end as soon as he got his chance to go to London. He gave the old woman his salary of the last three months. She tied it in the fold of her skirt and went back to the village.

Boota stuck to his job. Often he felt tired of sitting. Unused to sedentary life, he would shoot off to the *bazaar* or to the market on the slightest pretext and wander about. Once he stayed off duty the whole day. The matter was reported to the manager of the household and then to the higher authorities. Boota was summoned, sharply rebuked, and threatened that if he left his post again, he would be summarily dismissed. Then there would be no possibility of his going to the athletic tournaments ever.

It frightened Boota. He blinked his timid eyes and promised to behave more responsibly in future. After the warning he become punctual and cautious.

A year later, I went to Patiala to appear as a witness in a case before the judicial court. After a tiring day, I was standmg on the road, waiting for some conveyance when I saw a cycle-rickshaw slowly approaching. Beside it hobbled an old woman with a stick. When the rickshaw came nearer I recognised Boota sitting in it. He was wearing near khaki shorts and fine leather shoes. His shirt and turban were new. He greeted me with a smile and the driver halted the rickshaw.

'How are you, Boota?' I asked.

'By God's grace and your kindness I am quite well, thank you,' he replied. 'His Highness is away at Chail, his summer place. As soon as he comes back, I will be granted an interview. My name is at the top of the list... I hear an athletic team is going to London in the autumn. I hope to be selected...'

I looked at him and asked why he was riding in a rickshaw.

The old woman heaved a sigh and moaned, 'Oh, my son! My Boota was a free bird. Eternal sitting on a watchman's stool has been hard on him. Blood has curdled in his thighs and has gathered in his knees. Look, how swollen they are! Oh, my heart!'

She beat her breast with her fists and wailed, 'Now I am taking him to the hospital to have his knees treated.'

I looked at Boota. His once shield-like knees were now puffed and bulging.

He looked at me with his animal eyes. His lips opened like a freshly ploughed furrow and he said, 'The doctor is treating me with electric instruments. In a week my knees will be healed and I shall be able to run. Then sir, I'll go to London and run a hundred miles race...'

The rickshaw slowly crawled along and I stood there watching the mother and the son till they were lost in the distant curve of the road.

the night of the full moon

Kartar Singh Duggal

No one believed that Malan and Minnie were mother and daughter; they looked like sisters, Minnie was quite a bit taller than her mother. People said, 'Malan, your daughter has grown into a lovely woman!' They never stopped gaping at the girl. She was like a pearl and as charming as she was comely.

When Malan looked at her daughter she felt as if she was looking at herself. She too had been as young and as beautiful. She hadn't aged much either. And there was somebody who was willing to go to the ends of the earth for her even now.

Why had her mind wandered to this man? He must be a dealer in pearls because every time she thought of him pearls dropped from her eyes! Her daughter was now a woman; it was unbecoming of her to think of a man. She had restrained herself all these years; why did her mind begin to waver? She must hold herself in check. Her daughter was due to wed in another week; she must not entertain such evil thoughts — never! never!

'My very own, my dearest,' he had written only yesterday 'do not forget me.' But every time he came to the village she sent him away without any encouragement. She shut her eyes as fast as she shut her door against him. He had refused to give her up. She was his life; without her he found no peace. He had spent many years waiting for her, pleading with her, suffering the pangs of love and passion. An age had passed and now the afternoon shadows had lengthened across life's courtyard.

Malan knew in her heart that he would come that night. Every full moon lit night he knocked on her door. And tonight the moon would be full. The night would be cold, frosty and still. She had never unlatched her door for him. Would she tonight? She recalled a cold, moonlit night of many years ago. She was dancing in the mango grove when her *duppatta* had got caught in his hand. She had come to him bare-headed with the moonlight flecking her face with jasmine petals. He had put the *duppatta* across her shoulders — exactly the way it lay across her shoulders now. A shiver ran down Malan's spine.

Minnie came down the lane, tall and as slender as a cypress. Fair and fragile, she looked as if the touch of a human hand would leave a stain on her. Modestly, she had her *duppatta* wrapped round her face, and her eyes lowered.

Minnie was returning from the temple. She had prayed to the gods, she said softly to her mother, to grant her wish. She had prayed to the gods to grant everybody all their wishes.

Malan smiled. Something stirred her fancy. If her wish could be granted, she thought to herself, what would she ask for?

'Father has not returned!' complained Minnie.

'He is not expected back today; it will be a thousand blessings if he gets back by tomorrow. He has a lot of things to buy. At weddings and feasts it's better to have a little more than to run short,' explained Malan.

Minnie took off her sequined *duppatta* and spread it on her mother's shoulders. She took her mother's plain *duppatta*, instead and went into the kitchen.

The light of the full moon came through the branches and sprinkled itself on Malan's face. The full moon always did something to her. It made her feel like one drunk. In another four days women would come to her courtyard to sing wedding songs. They would put *henna* on the palms and the soles of her daughter's feet. They would help her with her bridal clothes; load her with ornaments. How would her daughter look in bright red silk? And then the groom would come on horseback and take her to his own home and make love to her. He would kiss the *henna* away from the girl's palms and the soles of her feet.

It wasn't so very long ago that all this had happened to her, Malan. But Minnie's father had not once kissed the soles of her feet, nor ever pressed her palms against his eyes. He always came home tired; he ate his meal and fell fast asleep. Only the desire to have a son would occasionally arouse him at midnight. And then it was over so quickly that Malan had to spend hours counting the stars to cool down and get back to sleep. These midnight efforts had produced a daughter every year. The girls came to the world uninvited and departed without leave. Only one, Minnie remained. She was the replica of her mother; like the fruit of a tree that bears only one. Minnie had large gazelle eyes — the eyes of Malan. Her long black hair fell down to her waist. And she had a full-bosomed wantoness which often made Malan think that all her frustrated passions had been rekindled in her daughter's body.

Minnie scrubbed the kitchen utensils, bolted the door of the courtyard and went to bed in her own room. Malan was left alone.

It was late. The moon was so dazzlingly bright that it seemed to be focussing all its light in that one courtyard. Was it cold? Not really. Just pleasantly cool. Malan asked herself why she sat alone in the courtyard under the night of the full moon. Was she expecting someone? Minnie had gone to bed and her father had gone away to the city. Why was he away on a night like this? On full moon nights she used to keep herself indoors away from temptation. But tonight she had her daughter's sequined *duppatta* wrapped about her face. The sequins glistened in the silvery moonlight; it seemed as if the stars were entangled in her hair; they twinkled on her eyelashes, on her face and on her shoulders. A night-jar called from the mango grove: *uk, uk, uk.* It would call like that all through the night — *uk, uk, uk.*

Her thoughts carried her with them. Her daughter would be married in a week's time. Then she would be left alone — all alone in the huge courtyard. A shiver ran through her body. The empty courtyard would terrify her. She would have to learn to live by herself. Her husband was too occupied with the pursuit of money; his money-lending and debt-collecting. He came back late in the evening only to collapse on his charpoy. She had often asked him why he involved himself in so many affairs, but it had not made any difference.

Malan went indoors and saw her daughter fast asleep — as dead to the world as only the young can be. Her red bangles lay beside her pillow. Silly girl! She had only to turn in her sleep and they would be crushed. Malan picked them up to put them on the mantelpiece. Before she knew it, she had slipped them on her own arms; six on one, six on the other. They glistened even in the dark. They were new; her daughter had only bought them the day before from the bangle-seller.

Malan came out in the moonlit courtyard — the sequined *duppatta* on her head and her arms a-jingle-jangle with bright red glass bangles. She felt like a bride — warm, lusty. Blood surged in her veins.

There was a gentle knock on the door. It was he. It was the same knock — a nervous, hesitant knock. He was there as he had written in his letter he would be: 'On the full moonlit night of December, I will knock at your door. If you are willing, open the door; if you are not willing, let it be. I will continue to knock at your door as I have always done.'

Knock, knock, knock — very soft, very sweet, a very inviting knock. Who could it be but he! The prowler in the moonlit nights. Suddenly the moon went behind a cloud and it was absolutely dark.

In a moment, Malan's feet took her across the dark courtyard. With trembling hands she undid the latch. Another moment and she was in his arms. Their lips met; their teeth ground against each other. Passion that had been held in check for over twenty years burst its banks and carried them on the flood.

Malan did not know how they went to the bo tree outside the village. She did not remember how they went into the field beside the bo tree — nor how long they stayed there. She was woken by the train which passed by the village in the early hours of the dawn. She extricated herself from her lover's embrace, covered her face with her *duppatta* and hurried back to her home.

She slipped off the bangles from her arms and put them back beside her daughter's pillow. She folded her daughter's sequined *duppatta,* took her own back and went to her charpoy. She fell asleep at once and slept as she had never slept before — almost as if she were making up for a lifetime of sleeplessness.

When she woke, the sun was streaming into the courtyard.

'How you slept, like a little babe!' teased Minnie. Minnie had swept the rooms and the courtyard and cooked the morning meal. She had bathed and was ready to go to the temple. She had tied jasmine flowers in her *duppatta* to offer to the gods.

As soon as Minnie left, Malan stretched herself lazily on a charpoy in the courtyard. She was filled with sleep and her head was filled with dreams.

A soft breeze began to blow. Warm sunshine spread in the courtyard. Malan felt like a bowl of milk, full to the brim — with a few petals of jasmine floating on it. It was a strange heady intoxication. Her eyes would close, open, and then close again.

'O Malan! Where's that slut?' cried a voice suddenly. Malan felt as if someone had slapped her face.

'Never heard of such goings on!' said another voice, 'and only four days to her wedding!'

'What has my daughter done?' shrieked Malan rising up in anger. 'She is as innocent as a calf.'

There were derisive exclamations. Then someone sneered, 'Your little calf has been on the dung heap all night.'

Malan's body went cold, her life-blood draining from her veins; a deathly pallor spread over her face.

Lajo, her neighbour, was speaking. 'It was barely dark when the bitch walked off with a stranger. I had got up to relieve myself when I saw them go away into the fields, with their arms entwined around each other's waists. I didn't get a wink of sleep. We have to watch the interests of our daughters. I've never heard of anyone blacken the faces of her parents in this way.'

Malan sat still as if turned to stone. She did not seem to hear what was being said.

The village watchman took up Lajo's story.

'Sister-in-law, Malan,' he said trying to attract her attention.

'What is it, Jumma?' Her voice seemed to come out of the depths of a deep well.

'*Bhabhi*, this is not the sort of thing one can talk about easily. An awful thing happened in the village last night. My hair has gone grey with the years I've been watchman of the village, but never have I known such a scandal. Your daughter blackened her face with someone under the bo tree. Twice I passed within ten paces of them. There they were locked together, limb joined to limb; oblivious of all but each other. I kept guard over your house. I said to myself "The wedding is to take place in another four days; the house must be full of new dresses and ornaments and the door wide open!" I left at dawn. I don't know what time your daughter came back after whoring. If she were my child I would break every bone in her body.'

Malan gazed at the watchman, stunned.

Jumma was followed by Ratna, the *zemindar*. He was in a rage.

'Where is that slut?' he roared. 'Couldn't she find another field for whoring?' Ratna leapt about as he spoke. The neighbours came out of their homes to watch and listen. Ratna continued. 'I was on my way to the well when I saw her come out of the field with her face wrapped in the sequined *duppatta*. I thought that the girl had come out to ease herself; but then her lover emerged from the other end of the same field. I saw them with my own eyes.'

At that moment, Minnie tore her way through the crowd. She had heard all that had been said about her. 'You are lying, uncle!' she shrieked.

'You dare call me a liar, you little trollop! You ill starred wretch! And how did a broken red bangle happen to be in my field?' He untied the knot in his shawl, took out a piece of red bangle and slapped it on Minnie's palm. Minnie ran her eyes over her arms and counted the bangles; there were only eleven. The world swam before her eyes and then darkened.

The women exchanged glances. They had seen Minnie buy the bangles. Yes, there were ten and then two more. And she had specially asked for red ones.

The courtyard was full of babbling men and women. Minnie's fiancee's father edged his way through; his wife was behind him. They flung all the presents they had received in front of Malan; clothes, money and rings. The crowd gaped. Women touched their ears; young girls bit their finger nails. This was drama indeed. A broken engagement was a broken life. What would Minnie do, now that she would never find a husband? It served her right, shameless harlot!

Over the sound of their angry droning, there was a loud splash. For a moment the crowd was petrified. Then someone shouted, 'The well!' and understanding dawned.

Minnie was nowhere to be seen. The gentle Minnie who never raised her voice against anyone, who was as pure as the jasmine she wove into garlands. Minnie, who never tired of praying to her gods for the happiness of everyone she knew.

Suddenly sobered, people ran to the well. Only Malan sat where she was, numb with horror, unable to move. Her courtyard was empty — emptier than it ever had been, as empty as it always would be now.

hunger

Krishen Singh Dhodi

It was the silver jubilee week of 'The Blood of the Lover' at the Nishat; the film had drawn a packed house for every showing of the preceding twenty-five weeks. That was not suprising as everyone has at one time or the other been in love; and everyone loved the film because they found their own life-story projected on the screen. The producer decided to celebrate the success by taking out a triumphal procession through the streets of the city. The publicity campaign was entrusted to a contractor, Sundar Singh.

Sundar Singh was a pleasant man of about forty-five. He lived in a house close by the Nishat. He lived alone because he did not have a relative in the world to share his home. He had employed a fifteen year old lad, Bachana Singh, to cook his meals for him. Bachana Singh gave his master the morning and the evening meal and spent the rest of the day parading through the streets sandwiched between cinema placards. For this he was paid Rs. 25 per month — all of which he gave to his widowed mother who lived in a refugee encampment.

The procession of the film 'The Blood of the Lover' started from the Nishat cinema at 8 a.m. Sundar Singh wore a bright red turban with starched plumes flaunting in the air. He carried a flag in his hand and ran up and down the procession shouting instructions. Heading the procession was Master Raja Lal's brass band. Following the band was a truck bearing mammoth-size portraits of the stars of the film; one picture showed a fountain of blood pouring out of the heart of the lover and falling at the feet of his sweetheart. Following the truck were a row of bullock-carts decorated with hoardings; following the bullock-carts were sandwichmen; and last of all were little urchins carrying sticks with placards stuck to them. Amongst the urchins was Bachana Singh.

Bachana Singh wore a clean shirt and pyjama; he had even polished his shoes. But there was no sign of joy on his face. He trudged on silently in the last rank with his eyes downcast and an age-old melancholy in his drooping visage. And there was his employer Sundar Singh, strutting about with the airs of a Field Marshall now commanding the band to play another air; now ordering the bullock cart drivers to keep in line; and again bellowing at the little boys to march in step.

It was a grand spectacle. Although the procession had been organised by the rich, the people who marched in it were poor — the poor who had agreed to tramp through dusty streets to be able to fill their bellies. Anyone pausing to see their pale, emaciated faces would have concluded that the procession was intended to advertise poverty — poverty which had celebrated a hundred thousand silver and golden jubilees.

The procession entered the city. It went along the main thoroughfare, the Mall, past the city's biggest bakery. The bakery bore a large sign-board picturing a giant-size loaf with the legend 'Delbis.' Bachana Singh's eyes fell on the picture; his mouth filled with saliva; he ran his tongue over his lips. He stopped in front of the bakery and stood entranced gaping at the board. Sundar Singh's harsh voice pierced through his eardrum. '*Oi Bachania! oi,* you son of a witch! keep moving.'

Bachana Singh ran to catch up with his rank. But his thoughts stayed behind with the loaf of bread. He marched on with the procession; his mind stuck to the hoarding; his feet went one way, his heart the other. He pondered over the hard life he led.

Bachana Singh got up at six every morning to give his master breakfast consisting of tea, toast cut out of a small loaf of Delbis and half a pat of butter. Sundar Singh used up all the butter and the bread leaving only the crust of the toast for his servant — this Bachana washed down with his own cup of tea. It was Bachana Singh's dream that one day he would eat a whole loaf of Delbis with a pat of butter. Since he gave his wages to his mother, there was nothing to spare for luxuries such as these. Once when Sundar Singh had felt a little under the weather, he had taken only one toast and given the rest of the loaf to his servant. Bachana still cherished the memory of that day and prayed that his master would again be indisposed and the entire loaf and the pat of butter would fall to the servant's share. The picture in the bakery made him so ravenously hungry that he imagined himself swallowing the entire loaf in one big gulp.

After breakfast Sundar Singh used to stroke his paunch and repeat: 'Great Guru, Emperor True! I thank Thee a hundred thousand times. Guru Gobind, Lord of the Plumes, all that Thy humble servant gets is but Thy gift; Thou givest and Thy humble servant's hunger is appeased'. And then Sundar Singh would emit a long, satisfied belch.

Bachana heard these words of thanksgiving every morning. How strange, he wondered, that the True Emperor should give to some and not to others! That He should give Sundar Singh a whole loaf with butter every day and him only the leftover crust! Silk shirts to Sundar Singh and tattered rags to Bachana! And then poor Bachana Singh would resume his breakfast of dry crust dipped in tea.

Sometimes Bachana asked himself why he had never thanked the Guru, the True Emperor. So one day he blurted out: 'Great Guru, True Emperor! For what I have received I thank Thee a hundred thousand times!' And immediately after he had uttered the words he felt a little silly; what had he to thank the Guru for? Just for the dry crust of bread? The thanks were due from Sundar Singh because he did get a whole loaf and butter every day. If he (Bachana) gave thanks for the crust, that's all the Guru would ever give him!

Once Sundar Singh went off toast for a few days; he began to take milk instead for his breakfast. Poor Bachana was deprived even of his scrap of toast. No wonder the mere picture of a loaf of bread made him drool at the mouth. He resolved to buy the bread and the butter; but where was the money to come from?

When he returned home after parading the streets, he was very tired. His limbs ached, and the longing for bread and butter gnawed at his inside. His master, Sundar Singh came back, changed into a suit and left to go to a reception given by the producer of the 'The Blood of the Lover.'

Bachana Singh had no means of raising a loan; he had asked his companion on the parade to give him eight *annas* but no one would lend the money; perhaps they were as hard up as he. Or did they suspect he would never be able to return the loan? Bachana tried to get a loaf and butter from the cinema restaurant; that also failed. Sundar Singh had given instructions that nothing was to be given on credit to his servant. Bachana Singh lay down on his charpoy. He was hungry.

Before he fell asleep, Bachana said a short prayer — his heart was too full for more. He hadn't asked for a million rupees or motor cars or bungalows — only a small loaf of bread and half a pat of butter. Even that was denied him! He prayed fervently. 'Great Guru, True Emperor, I have forsaken others and come to Your door. People say You are the Great Giver. I too have seen Your generosity towards the proprietor of the Nishat cinema and to contractor Sundar Singh. But why give You not to me and a hundred thousand others like me? Who else can we turn to? If You really are the Great Giver, then give Your servant a loaf of bread. Otherwise I will conclude that You are the Guru of the chosen few and I shall find a new Guru of my own.' Bachana Singh's eyes closed in sleep.

Late in the night he awoke with an eerie feeling. His room was lit with strange effulgence. A bright glittering figure dismounted from a horse and entered his room. A white hawk fluttered on his hand. Of course, it was Guru Govind Singh Himself! Bachana rushed and bowed his head to the Guru's feet and then offered the Guru his humble three-legged stool. The guru embraced Bachana.

'My son, you thought of me in your prayers!'

'Yes, Father!' replied Bachana folding the palms of his hands and dropping his eyes.

'Why did you think of me, son?' asked the Guru with great kindness.

'Emperor True! You know the innermost secrets of our hearts; You know of my suffering!'

'Son, ask what you wish and it will be granted.' Bachana remained silent.

'Son, be not shy! Ask for what your heart wills most.'

'Emperor True! Will You really give me what I ask?'

'Yes son; you thought of me in the truthfulness of your heart. For this whatever your heart wills will be granted.'

'Give me a small loaf of Delbis and half a pat of butter,' blurted Bachana smacking his lips.

'A loaf of Delbis and half a pat of butter! Four and three — that is only seven *annas* worth per day! Son, know the status of the one who gives and then ask. Ask for happiness in this life and the life to come; ask for dominion over the globe and I shall grant it to you; I can make you King of the three worlds.'

'No my Lord! I do not want dominion or power. It was different in your age; today King's heads roll in the dust and are kicked about by common people. All I need is a loaf of bread. And many who are as poor as I also need bread. I do not wish to own a kingdom; but I also do not want to spend a lifetime in hunger and want. Appease my hunger in this life; I will not bother about life hereafter.'

'You will get all you want and quite soon in the life to come you will have everything in full measure. I will have to come back to this world again; not to save India from the perils of a foreign invasion but to give every Indian bread and butter. Wait for my return.'

'True Emperor! I have waited long. Don't take more time, come as soon as you can.'

'I will not be long.'

The effulgent figure remounted the horse and vanished.

'*Oi Bachania!* Get up you lazy lout! Its almost afternoon and you are still in bed. Get up and get my Delbis and butter.'

Bachana had gone to bed very late; then there was that strange dream! When he heard the word Delbis, he rose with a start — but still in his dream world.

'True Emperor! You have really come — and sooner than you promised! Where is my Delbis and my pat of butter?'

62

Sundar Singh gave the boy a quizzical glance. '*Oi*, whose father are you talking to? You didn't drug yourself with hashish, did you? Do I get the breakfast for you, or you for me? Hurry up you slug-a-bed and get my Delbis and butter.'

'Someone there is who is going to get Delbis and butter for me; soon, very soon.'

Bachana opened his eyes. Sundar Sigh stood glowering over him. Bachana quickly shut his eyes and stretched himself on the charpoy again.

Sundar Singh picked up the charpoy from one end and tilted it over. Bachana rolled off and fell on the floor.

gods on trial

Gulzar Singh Sandhu

Noora sat quietly under a mango tree by the tombs of the *Pirs*. He was absorbed in doing the home task given by his teacher. Rahmte, his sister, was cutting fodder from the Sikh Martyrs' field, near the *Pirs'* graveyard.

The Martyrs entombed near our field are supposed to possess great miraculous powers transcending death, fire and time. We, of the Sikh religion have profound faith in them. So much so that I was not allowed even to take the school examination unless I pledged an offering to them. My grandfather believed that it was only because of the Martyr's kind intercession that I never once failed in any examination.

That summer day, I was also sitting with Noora under the mango tree. While Noora was engrossed in homework I watched Rahmte, cutting fodder from our field. I liked her so much that I felt like talking about her to Noora.

'Of your two sisters whom do you like more? Rahmte or Jaina?' I asked.

'Jaina,' he said, naming the elder one that had been married for four years then.

'Why don't you like Rahmte?' said I and was suddenly aware that I could be misunderstood.

'She beat me once, which Jaina never did,' he said casually, to my satisfaction and returned to his book. Assured that I was not misunderstood, I started watching the rhythmic movement of Rahmte's limbs operating the sickle.

Just then something startled a peacock on the Martyrs' *peepul* tree, and it shot off into the air flapping its large wings with a heavy, muffled thud-thud. One of the feathers came off and sailed down to the ground. I was then a keen collector of peacock feathers. As I saw one sailing down in its rich dazzling colours, I threw down my book and ran for it. But it never touched the ground. Rahmte had grabbed it from the air before I could.

'Hand it to me,' I said a little tensely.

'I got it first,' she replied coldly.

'None of that!' I threatened, 'You have to give it to me.'

'Oh, I have to, have I?' she scoffed. 'In that case I shan't!'

'Come on, hand it over and I'll never ask anything more from you.' I tried to sound suggestive and grown up. She flushed.

'Take it, there,' she said curtly throwing the feather away. She collected the fodder into a sheaf, picked it up and started home. I could not take my eyes from her slender figure, straining under the weight of the sheaf. I was left wondering whether I had really offended her.

Back in the graveyard I found Noora's father the saintly Badru, saying his *namaaz*. Noora stood by humbly. Both the father and the son had incongruous yellow scarves, the symbol of the Sikh religion, around their necks, for they, along with others, had recently agreed to 'conversion.' These were the days of communal riots and the yellow scarf guaranteed security to the Muslim minority in East Punjab.

The Partition of the country had torn India into two parts and conversion had been made a condition by the Sikhs, for those Muslims staying on in India, in retaliation to a similar declaration by Muslims in Pakistan for any Hindus or Sikhs there. The majority, no doubt, in our area were Muslims, and that too of the orthodox sect of Sunnis. But what could they do? They were in India and whoever did not convert to Sikhism was killed.

After the invitation for conversion a huge number of steel bangles, wooden crescent combs and yellow scarves were procured for an elaborate conversion ceremony. Just when the *parsad,* the sanctified sweet, was being prepared for initiating the Muslims to the Sikh religion, a phlegmatic voice said:

'What good is this initiation, bound by outward symbols? These cannot deter them from continuing to be Muslims at heart!' It was Baba Phuman Singh, pausing to fling a pellet of opium into the hollow cavern of his mouth.

'What else do you advise us to do?'

'Feed them with pork,' he said.

'Our own people have been made to eat beef on that side of the border,' said another.

Everyone agreed to feed pork to the Muslims gathered for initiation. Four or five pigs were killed and cooked immediately. This ceremony had been carried out in a similar manner in neighbouring villages also.

The Muslims listened and watched with the resigned passivity and indifference of those who no longer cared whether they live or die.

'Our Gurus baptised with *parsad* only,' my father whispered to *Babaji,* in mild protest.

'Keep your mouth shut, man. Nothing like silence,' he said and drifted towards the pots of meat to examine the quality.

66

In a little while all the Muslims were initiated into the Sikh religion. Wearing the five symbols of Sikhism they started swallowing the pieces of pork served to them.

'We have always been Hindus. Only that blasted Aurangzeb made us change,' one of them said in a futile effort to seek justification for his acts. *Babaji* and a jew other village elders, sat a little separately from the rest, in their own superior elite group of Sandhus.

'The Maharaja of Patiala is a Sidhu,' I heard him say. 'Sidhu and Sandhu are equal. The only difference is that our *jagir* provides us only with opium while the maharaja's gives him all the luxury he could dream of.' The talk did not interest me.

'Noora and his people are not being baptised?' I asked my father. 'Hush!' my father silenced me, 'I have delivered all the five symbols to them and they are wearing them. Noora's father is a saintly person and respects us. I wouldn't want him to feel disgraced in public. May be he does not want to take part.'

When my grandfather asked about the baptism of Badru and his family, my father managed to convince him that Badru had taken pork in his very presence. To allay any remaining doubts, father swore it solemnly and thus the whole of Badru's family was also counted among the baptised.

And where was the lie in it? That day when I had demanded the peacock feather from Rahmte she was wearing a yellow *duppatta* on her head and a steel bangle on her wrist. Her father Badru and her brother Noora too were wearing yellow scarves around their necks and steel bangles on their wrists. Both were performing the *namaaz*. They would not have dared to pray the Muslim way had there been a witness. But then the only person present was myself and I was his pupil. They knew well that I would not tell anyone in the village that they were praying the Muslim way. How could I, who till the third standard had done my sums with the help of Rahmte?

It is still all so clear before my eyes, that day — Rahmte carrying the sheaf of fodder, Badru and Noora praying. The long *henna*-dyed beard of the holy man touched the ground as he bowed in prayer. His loose *lucknawi* shirt was a little dirty. I stood at some distance watching them all, when I heard sudden shouts of *'Bole so nihal, sat sri akal.'* It was the Sikh cry and it sent us running for our lives in great terror. In the general panic Noora stumbled and fell on the ground. The running hoofs came to a stop and many a spear was jabbed viciously into his body. He lay there with his entrails hanging out. It was the last I saw of him.

I looked at the riders in yellow and blue and stood there dazed. They had already closed in on Badru. The saint pleaded with folded hands flourishing his yellow scarf and the steel bangle on his wrist to show he was a Sikh. A Nihang Sikh with fox-tail moustaches, playfully struck the wrist which was raised to exhibit the bangle, and cut it clean from the elbow. When Badru raised his other hand in abject imploration, the tyrant struck that off too.

'Send this pig as well to Pakistan,' someone shouted and ran towards me.

Sending one to Pakistan was a common phrase for killing a Muslim.

'He's a Sikh one, you fool,' a voice checked him. It was the Nihang Sikh who had speared Noora.

From his saddle he lifted me up and put me in his lap.

I do not know what happened after that, for I lost consciousness.

When I came to my senses next day I was lying in bed in the verandah. My mother's eyes were red and swollen with crying.

'He's saved, don't you worry. It was only shock. He is just a child after all.' *Babaji* was talking to my mother.

'It was almost the end of him,' my mother said wiping her tears and rubbing my limbs.

'What a dreadful shock for you, my son! God protect you, God bless you,' she said wiping my face with her *duppatta*.

'Bless and be blessed afterwards, first give offerings to the Martyrs who saved his life,' said *Babaji* and everyone agreed to this proposal. They started making preparations for the Martyrs.

Chokingly, I told my mother about Noora's death and asked her in a trembling voice if she knew anything about Rahmte. She told me in tears that Jaina and Rahmte were abducted by the crusading rioters along with other Muslim girls of the village. Many were murdered, about fifty of them. Whoever was seen with a new yellow scarf and bright steel bangle was killed.

Meanwhile the whole of the village made ready to offer *parsad* to the Martyrs. Though it was a quiet evening, everyone was frightened. Baba Phuman Singh was absolutely stunned. He was almost out of his wits. Just a while ago he was informed that his life-long friend Ghanshamdas had also been killed by mistake. He had been carrying a yellow scarf to one of his Muslim friends out in the fields, when he was surprised by the rioters who killed him, taking him to be a new convert. They did not wait to check who was who. They were busy people. They had to visit and plunder other villages too. For them the sight of a yellow scarf was enough to tell them of 'converts.'

While praying at the Martyrs field, *Babaji* (my grandfather) was still thinking of Ghanshamdas. Yes, true, he had to die some day. But this sudden and uncalled for death had given a new uncertainty to people, including *Babaji*. It meant that anyone who was carrying a yellow scarf, even if he was a

Sikh or a Hindu, would not be spared. Where then was the guarantee of safety to converts? In fact those who had not accepted Sikhism were safer, for they were cautious, not caught so easily and hence not killed. Thus, absurdly, avowed Muslims were escaping while Sikhs were being slaughtered!

Even though he was singing aloud the praises of Guru Gobind's sons, the Five Beloved Ones, and the Forty Martyrs, his heart was crying over the calamitous riots towards the end when he was reciting verses in honour of those who had shared their wealth, fought sinners, offered sacrifice for the faith, suddenly his legs buckled beneath him. The mention of 'sacrifices for the faith' choked his throat. His *khunda* fell off on the ground. The rest of the prayer was completed by my father. Having finished the ceremony my father told me to go and offer *parsad* to the Martyrs. As I placed the *parsad* on their tombs, the crows from the *peepul* tree nearby came cawing and swooping and ate it up in no time. 'Let the Martyrs remain hungry,' I said to myself.

As my father distributed *parsad* to everyone and was about to leave, *Babaji* came forward and held him there by his arm.

'Tell the boy to put some on the *Pirs* tombs too,' he said pointing towards the *Pirs'* graveyard. Looking in that direction I remembered Noora. The *peepul* in the field reminded me of Rahmte who had frowned at me under it. Had she done it in love or in hatred? I would never know now.

'What do you mean?' father asked *Babaji,* a little puzzled — 'on the *Pirs'* tombs?'

'You remember the massacre,' *Babaji* whispered to father, after taking him beyond the boundary of the field. Perhaps he dared not say it within the Martyrs' domain, afraid of their curse on his unbelief.

'Yes, I remember,' father said bitterly.

'Those who were initiated have been killed, haven't they?'

'So what?' whispered my father still puzzled.

'Those who did not agree to initiation are saved, you know that.'

'I don't understand,' father said, frowning perplexedly. 'Well, if you don't, I can't help it,' snapped *Babaji,* a little irritated by my father's denseness.

'Listen,' he tried again, whispering very low to prevent the Martyrs overhearing. 'Those who remained Muslims were saved, were they not? Well, who knows if tomorrow the *Pirs* don't turn out to be more powerful than our Martyrs?'

Suddenly enlightened, I ran and offered *parsad* at the *Pirs'* tombs. Father did not stop me.

Perhaps the insinuation in *Babaji's* remarks still escaped him?

the death of shaikh burhanuddin

Khwaja Ahmed Abbas

My name is Shaikh Burhanuddin.

When violence and murder became the order of the day in Delhi and the blood of Muslims flowed in the streets, I cursed my fate for having a Sikh for a neighbour. Far from expecting him to come to my rescue in times of trouble, as a good neighbour should, I could not tell when he would thrust his *kirpan* into my belly. The truth is that till then I used to find the Sikhs somewhat laughable. But I also disliked them and was somewhat scared of them.

My hatred for the Sikhs began on the day when I first set my eyes on one. I could not have been more than six years old when I saw a Sikh sitting out in the sun combing his long hair. 'Look!' I yelled with revulsion, 'a woman with a long beard!' As I got older this dislike developed into hatred for the entire race.

It was a custom amongst old women of our household to heap all afflictions on our enemies. Thus, for example, if a child got pneumonia or broke its leg, they would say 'a long time ago a Sikh, (or an Englishman), got pneumonia: or a long time ago a Sikh, (or an Englishman), broke his leg'. When I was older I discovered that this referred to the year 1857 when the Sikh princes helped the *ferringee* foreigner — to defeat the Hindus and Muslims in the War of Independence. I do not wish to propound a historical thesis but to explain the obsession, the suspicion and hatred which I bore towards the English and the Sikhs. I was more frightened of the English than of the Sikhs.

When I was ten years old, I happened to be travelling from Delhi to Aligarh. I used to travel third class, or at the most in the intermediate class. That day I said to myself, 'Let me for once travel second class and see what it feels like.' I bought my ticket and I found an empty second class compartment. I jumped on the well-sprung seats; I went into the bathroom and leapt up to see my face in the mirror; I switched on all the fans. I played with the light switches. There were only a couple of minutes for the train to leave when four red-faced 'tommies' burst into the compartment, mouthing obscenities: everything was either 'bloody' or 'damn.' I had one look at them and my desire to travel second class vanished.

I picked up my suitcase and ran out. I only stopped for breath when I got into a third class compartment crammed with natives. But as luck would have it it was full of Sikhs — their beards hanging down to their navels and dressed in nothing more than their underpants. I could not escape from them: but I kept my distance.

Although I feared the white man more than the Sikhs, I felt that he was more civilised: he wore the same kind of clothes as I. I also wanted to be able to say 'damn', 'bloody fool' — the way he did. And like him I wanted to belong to the ruling class. The Englishman ate his food with forks and knives, I also wanted to learn to eat with forks and knives so that natives would look upon me as advanced and as civilised as the whiteman.

My Sikh-phobia was of different kind. I had contempt for the Sikh. I was amazed at the stupidity of men who imitated women and grew their hair long. I must confess I did not like my hair cut too short; despite my father's instructions to the contrary, I did not allow the barber to clip off more than a little

73

when I went to him on Fridays. I grew a mop of hair so that when I played hockey or football it would blow about in the breeze like those of English sportsmen. My father often asked me, 'Why do you let your hair grow like a woman's?' My father had primitive ideas and I took no notice of his views. If he had had his way he would have had all heads razored bald and stuck artificial beards on people's chins...That reminds me that the second reason for hating the Sikhs was their beards which made them look like savages.

There are beards and beards. There was my father's beard, neatly trimmed in the French style; or my uncle's which went into a sharp point under his chin. But what could you do with a beard to which no scissor was ever applied and which was allowed to grow like a wild bush — fed with a compost of oil, curd and goodness knows what! And, after it had grown a few feet, combed like hair on a head: My grandfather also had a very long beard which he combed... but then my grandfather was my grandfather and a Sikh is just a Sikh.

After I had passed my matriculation examination I was sent to the Muslim University at Aligarh. We boys who came from Delhi, or the United Provinces, looked down upon boys from Punjab; they were crude rustics who did not know how to converse, how to behave at table, or to deport themselves in polite company. All they could do was drink large tumblers of buttermilk. Delicacies such as vermicelli with essence of *kewra* sprinkled on it or the aroma of Lipton's tea were alien to them. Their language was unsophisticated to the extreme, whenever they spoke to each other it seemed as if they were quarreling. It was full of '*ussi, tussi, saadey, twhaadey,*' — Heaven forbid. I kept my distance from Punjabis.

But the warden of our hostel, (God forgive him), gave me a Punjabi as a roommate. When I realised that there was no escape, I decided to make the best of a bad bargain and be civil to the chap. After a few days we became quite friendly. This man was called Ghulam Rasul and he was from Rawalpindi. He was full of amusing anecdotes and was a good companion.

You might well ask how Mr. Ghulam Rasul gate-crashed into a story about the Sikhs. The fact of the matter is that Ghulam Rasul's anecdotes were usually about the Sikhs. It is through these anecdotes that I got to know the racial characteristics, the habits and customs of this strange community. According to Ghulam Rasul the chief characteristics of the Sikhs were the following:

All Sikhs were stupid and idiotic. At noontime they lost their senses altogether. There were many instances to prove this. For example, one day at 12 noon, a Sikh was cycling along Hall Bazaar in Amritsar when a constable, also a Sikh, stopped him and demanded, 'Where is your light?' The cyclist replied nervously, *Jemadar* Sahib, I lit it when I left my home; it must have gone out just now.' The constable threatened to run him in. A passer-by, yet another Sikh with a long white beard, intervened, 'Brothers, there is no point in quarrelling over little things. If the light has gone out it can be lit again.'

Ghulam Rasul knew hundreds of anecdotes of this kind. When he told them in his Punjabi accent his audience was left helpless with laughter. One really enjoyed them best in Punjabi because the strange and incomprehensible behaviour of the uncouth Sikh was best told in his rustic lingo.

The Sikhs were not only stupid but incredibly filthy as well. Ghulam Rasul, who had known hundreds of them, told us how they never shaved their heads. And whereas we Muslims washed our hair thoroughly at least every Friday, the Sikhs who made a public exhibition of bathing in their underpants, poured all kinds of filth, like curd into their hair. I rub lime-juice and glycerine in my scalp. Although the glycerine is white and thick like curd, it is an altogether different thing — made by a well-known firm of perfumers of Europe. My glycerine came in a lovely bottle whereas the Sikh's curd came from the shop of a dirty sweetmeat seller.

I would not have concerned myself with the manner of living of these people except that they were so haughty and ill-bred as to consider themselves as good warriors as the Muslims. It is known over the world that one Muslim can get the better of ten Hindus or Sikhs. But these Sikhs would not accept the superiority of the Muslim and would strut about like bantam cocks twirling their moustaches and stroking their beards. Ghulam Rasul used to say that one day we Muslims would teach the Sikhs a lesson that they would never forget.

Years went by.

I left college. I ceased to be a student and became a clerk; then a head clerk. I left Aligarh and came to live in New Delhi. I was allotted government quarters. I got married. I had children.

The quarters next to mine were occupied by a Sikh who had been displaced from Rawalpindi. Despite the passage of years, I remembered what Ghulam Rasul had told me. As Ghulam Rasul had prophesied, the Sikhs had been taught a bitter lesson in humility at least, in the district of Rawalpindi. The Muslims had virtually wiped them out. The Sikhs boasted that they were great heroes; they flaunted their long *kirpans*. But they could not withstand the brave Muslims. The Sikhs' beards were forcibly shaved. They were circumcised. They were converted to Islam. The Hindu press, as was its custom, vilified the Muslims. It reported that the Muslims had murdered Sikh woman and children. This was wholly contrary to Islamic tradition. No Muslim warrior was ever known to raise his hand against a woman or a child. The pictures of the corpses of women and children published in Hindu newspapers were obviously faked. I wouldn't have put it beyond the Sikh to murder their own women and children in order to vilify the Muslims.

The Muslims were also accused of abducting Hindu and Sikh women. The truth of the matter is that such was the impact of the heroism of Muslims on the minds of Hindu and Sikh girls that they fell in love with young Muslims and insisted on going with them. These noble-minded young men had no option but to give them shelter and thus bring them to the true path of Islam. The bubble of Sikh bravery was burst. It did not matter how their leaders threatened the Muslims with their *kirpans,* the sight of the Sikhs who had fled from Rawalpindi filled my heart with pride in the greatness of Islam.

The Sikh who was my neighbour was about sixty years old. His beard had gone completely grey. Although he had barely escaped from the jaws of death, he was always laughing, displaying his teeth in the most vulgar fashion. It was evident that he was quite stupid. In the beginning he tried to draw me into his net by professions of friendship. Whenever I passed him he insisted on talking to me. I do not remember what kind of Sikh festival it was, when he sent me some sweet butter. My wife promptly gave it away to the sweepress. I did my best to have as little to do with him as I could. I snubbed him whenever I could. I knew that if I spoke a few words to him, he would be hard to shake off. Civil talk would encourage him to become familiar. It was known to me that Sikhs drew their sustenance from foul language. Why should I soil my lips by associating with such people!

One Sunday afternoon I was telling my wife of some anecdotes about the stupidity of the Sikhs. To prove my point, exactly at 12 o'clock, I sent my servant across to my Sikh neighbour to ask him the time. He sent back the reply, 'Two minutes after 12.' I remarked to my wife 'You see, they are scared of even mentioning 12 o'clock!' We both had a hearty laugh. After this, many a time when I wanted to make an ass of my Sikh neighbour, I would ask him, 'Well, Sardarji has it struck twelve?' The shameless creature would grin, baring all his teeth and answer, 'Sir, for us it is always striking twelve.' He would roar with laughter as if it were a great joke.

I was concerned about the safety of my children. One could never trust a Sikh. And this man had fled from Rawalpindi. He was sure to have a grudge against Muslims and to be on the lookout for an opportunity to avenge himself. I had told my wife never to allow the children to go near the Sikh's quarters. But children are children. After a few days I saw my children playing with the Sikh's little girl, Mohini, and his other grandchildren. This child, who was barely ten years old, was really as beautiful as her name indicated; she was fair and beautifully formed. These wretches have beautiful women. I recall Ghulam Rasul telling me that if all the Sikh men were to leave their women behind and clear out of Punjab, there would be no need for Muslims to go to paradise in search of houris.

The truth about the Sikhs was soon evident. After the thrashing in Rawalpindi, they fled like cowards to East Punjab. Here they found the Muslims weak and unprepared. So they began to kill them. Hundreds of thousands of Muslims were martyred; the blood of the faithful ran in streams. Thousands of women were stripped naked and made to parade through the streets. When Sikhs, fleeing from Western Punjab, came in large numbers to Delhi, it was evident that there would be trouble in the capital. I could not leave for Pakistan immediately. Consequently I sent away my wife and children by air, with my elder brother, and entrusted my own fate to God. I could not send much luggage by air. I booked an entire railway wagon to take my furniture and belongings. But on the day I was to load the wagon I got information that trains bound for PakIstan were being attacked by Sikh bands. Consequently my luggage stayed in my quarters in Delhi.

On the 15th of August, India celebrated its independence. What interest could I have in the idependence of India! I spent the day lying in bed reading *Dawn* and the *Pakistan Times*. Both the papers had strong words to say about the manner in which India had gained its freedom and proved conclusively how the Hindus and the British had conspired to destroy the Muslims. It was only our leader, the great Mohammed Ali Jinnah, who was able to thwart their evil designs and win Pakistan for the Muslims. The English had knuckled under because of Hindu and Sikh pressure and handed over Amritsar to India. Amritsar, as the world knows, is a purely Muslim city. Its famous Golden Mosque — or am I mixing it up with the Golden Temple! — yes of course, the Golden Mosque there are the Jama Masjid, the Red Fort, the mausolea of Nizamuddin and Emperor Humayun, the tomb and school of Safdar Jang — just everything worthwhile bears imprints of Islamic rule. Even so this Delhi (which should really be called after its Muslim builder Shahjahan as Shahjahanabad) was to suffer the indignity of having the flag of Hindu imperialism unfurled on its ramparts.

My heart seemed rent asunder. I could have shed tears of blood. My cup of sorrow was full to the brim when I realised that Delhi, which was once the footstool of the Muslim Empire, the centre of Islamic culture and civilisation, had been snatched out of our hands. Instead we were to have the desert wastes of Western Punjab, Sindh and Baluchistan inhabited by an uncouth and uncultured people. We were to go to a land where people do not know how to talk in civilised Urdu; where men wear baggy *salwars* like their women folk, where they eat thick bread four pounds in weight instead of the delicate wafers we eat at home!

I steeled myself. I would have to make this sacrifice for my great leader, Jinnah, and for my new country, Pakistan.

Nevertheless the thought of having to leave Delhi was most depressing.

When I emerged from my room in the evening, my Sikh neighbour bared his fangs and asked, 'Brother, did you not go out to see the celebrations?' I felt like setting fire to his beard.

One morning the news spread of a general massacre in old Delhi. Muslim homes were burnt in Karol Bagh. Muslim shops in Chandni Chowk were looted. This then was a sample of Hindu rule! I said to myself, 'New Delhi is really an English city; Lord Mountbatten lives here as well as the Commander-in-Chief. At least in New Delhi no hand will be raised against Muslims.' With this self assurance I started towards my office. I had to settle the business of my provident fund; I had delayed going to Pakistan in order to do so. I had only got as far as Gole Market when I ran into a Hindu colleague in the office. He said, 'What on earth are you up to? Go back at once and do not come out of your house. The rioters are killing Muslims in Connaught Circus.' I hurried back home.

I had barely got to my quarters when I ran into my Sikh neighbour. He began to reassure me. 'Sheikhji, do not worry! As long as I am alive no one will raise a hand against you.' I said to myself: 'How much fraud is hidden behind this man's bread! He is obviously pleased that the Muslims are being massacred, but expresses sympathy to win my confidence; or is he trying to taunt me?' I was the only Muslim living in the block, perhaps I was the only one on the road.

I did not want these people's kindness or sympathy. I went inside my quarter and said to myself, 'If I have to die, I will kill at least ten or twenty men before they get me.' I went to my room where beneath my bed I kept my doublebarrelled gun. I had also collected quite a hoard of cartridges.

I searched the house, but could not find the gun.

'What is *huzoor* looking for?' asked my faithful servant, Mohammed.

'What happened to my gun?'

He did not answer. But I could tell from the way he looked that he had either hidden it or stolen it.

'Why don't you answer?' I asked him angrily.

Then he came out with the truth. He had stolen my gun and given it to some of his friends who were collecting arms to defend the Muslims in Daryaganj.

'We have hundreds of guns, several machine guns, ten revolvers and a cannon. We will slaughter these infidels; we will roast them alive.'

'No doubt with my gun you will roast the infidels in Daryaganj, but who will defend me here? I am the only Mussulman amongst these savages. If I am murdered, who will answer for it?'

I persuaded him to steal his way to Daryaganj to bring back my gun and couple of hundred cartridges. When he left I was convinced that I would never see him again. I was all alone. On the mantlepiece was a family photograph. My wife and children stared silently at me. My eyes filled with tears at the thought that I would never see them again. I was comforted with the thought that they were safe in Pakistan. Why had I been tempted by my paltry providend fund and not gone with them? I heard the crowd yelling.

'*Sat Sri Akal...*'

'*Har Har Mahadev.*'

The yelling came closer and closer. They were rioters — the bearers of my death warrant. I was like a wounded deer, running hither and thither, with the hunters' hounds in full pursuit. There was no escape. The door was made of very thin wood and glass panes. The rioters would smash their way in.

'Sat Sri Akal...'

'Har Har Mahadev.'

They were coming closer and closer; death was coming closer and closer. Suddenly there was a knock at the door. My Sikh neighbour walked in — *'Sheikhji,* come into my quarters at once.' Without a second thought I ran into the Sikh's verandah and hid behind the columns. A shot hit the wall above my head. A truck drew up and about a dozen young men climbed down. Their leader had a list in his hand — 'Quarter No. 8 — Sheikh Burhanuddin'. He read my name and ordered his gang to go ahead. They invaded my quarter and under my very eyes proceeded to destroy my home. My furniture, boxes, pictures, books, druggets and carpets, even the dirty linen was carried into the truck. Robbers! Thugs! Cut-throats!

As for the Sikh, who had pretended to sympathise with me, he was no less a robber than they! He was pleading with the rioters: 'Gentlemen, stop! We have prior claim over our neighbour's property. We must get our share of the loot.' He beckoned to his sons and daughters. All of them gathered to pick up whatever they could lay their hands on. One took my trousers; another a suitcase.

They even grabbed the family photograph. They took the loot to their quarters.

You bloody Sikh! If God grants me life I will settle my score with you. At this moment I cannot even protest. The rioters are armed and only a few yards away from me. If they get to know of my presence...

'Please come in.'

My eyes fell on the unsheathed *kirpan* in the hands of the Sikh. He was inviting me to come in. The bearded monster looked more frightful after he had soiled his hands with my property. There was the glittering blade of his *kirpan* inviting me to my doom. There was no time to argue. The only choice was between the guns of the rioters and the sabre of the Sikh. I decided, rather the *kirpan* of the old man than ten armed gangsters. I went into the room hesitantly, silently.

'Not here, come in further,' I went into the inner room like a goat following a butcher. The glint of the blade of the *kirpan* was almost blinding.

'Here you are, take your things,' said the Sikh.

He and his children put all the stuff they had pretended to loot, in front of me. His old woman said, 'Son, I am sorry we were not able to save more.'

I was dumb-founded.

The gangsters had dragged out my steel almirah and were trying to smash it open. 'It would be simpler if we could find the keys,' said someone.

'The keys can only be found in Pakistan. That cowardly son of a filthy Muslim has decamped,' replied another.

Little Mohini answered back: '*Sheikhji* is not a coward. He had not run off to Pakistan.'

'Where is he blackening his face?'

'Why should he be blackening his face? He is in...' Mohini realised her mistake and stopped in her sentence. Blood mounted in her father's face. He locked me in the inside room, gave his *kirpan* to his son and went out to face the mob.

I do not know what exactly took place outside. I heard the sound of blows; then Mohini crying; then the Sikh yelling full-blooded abuse in Punjabi. And then a shot and the Sikh's cry of pain '*hai.*'

I heard a truck engine starting up and then there was a petrified silence.

When I was taken out of my prison my Sikh neighbour was lying on a charpoy. Beside him lay a torn and bloodstained shirt. His new shirt also was oozing with blood. His son had gone to telephone for the doctor.

'Sardarji, what have you done?' I do not know how these words came out of my lips. The world of hate in which I had lived all these years, lay in ruins about me.

'Sardarji, why did you do this?' I asked him again.

'Son, I had a debt to pay.'

'What kind of a debt?'

'In Rawalpindi there was a Muslim like you who sacrificed his life to save mine and the honour of my family.'

'What was his name, Sardarji?'

'Ghulam Rasul.'

Fate had played a cruel trick on me. The clock on the wall started to strike... 1... 2... 3... 4... 5... The Sikh turned towards the clock and smiled. He reminded me of my grandfather with his twelve-inch beard. How closely the two resembled each other!

...6...7...8...9...We counted in silence.

He smiled again. His white beard and long white hair were like a halo, effulgent with a divine light... 10... 11... 12... The clock stopped striking.

I could almost hear him say: 'For us Sikhs, it is always 12 o'clock!'

But the bearded lips, still smiling, were silent. And I knew he was already in some distant world, where the striking of clocks counted for nothing, where violence and mockery were powerless to hurt him.

the mahabharata retold

Satindra Singh

Until the partition of the Indian subcontinent in August 1947, Gurdaspur was
a small town. Life crawled on without change, without
excitement. Its inhabitants were completely unaware of the
brightness of life.

True, there was some variety and colour in its otherwise
drab and seemingly changless existence when religious festivals
came. On Dussehra, there was some gaiety and pageantry when
the effigy of the demon king, Ravana, was burnt amidst the
deafening exploding of crackers. On Diwali, the festival of
earthen lamps, too, there was some commotion and some
excitement and some change in the ancient routine of life. Holi
was also celebrated with joyous abandon, with sprinkling of
colours and coloured water. On Baisakhi, the rustic and sturdy
peasants performed bhangra dances in order to celebrate the
coming of the harvest when the golden wheat swayed delicately
in the spring breeze.

The routine of life was also somewhat ruffled in a pleasant
way on the occasion of the birth anniversaries of Guru Nanak
Dev and Guru Gobind Singh. On these auspicious occasions,
robust and bearded Sikhs, naked swords in hand, led the
procession, heads bowed before the holy *Granth* carried
shoulder-high in a palanquin.

There was also some change in the lazy and colourless stream of life on Eid and Shab-e-baraat when puritanical Muslims let themselves go.

On all these occasions, flung far and few between, children put on new clothes and were allowed to while away their time — playing.

Besides these religious — and necessarily communal festivals — children had opportunities to celebrate common events without consideration of caste or community. Though not regular, such occasions were looked forward to with great keenness.

One of these was the arrival of the road-roller during the summer season. For us it was a day to keep away from school. We did not come home for our mid-day meals and the ordained siesta thereafter. All this, of course, meant the birch both at school and at home. But who cared? We exultingly followed the road-roller from one end of the main street to another. Its whistle sent us into ecstasy. We stopped our ears with our fingers, closed our eyes and felt lifted up and floating in the air.

The only thing that dwarfed the road-roller in our estimation was the arrival of a circus, a theatrical company or a touring cinema. For that was a completely new world for us. The arrival of anyone of these threw Gurdaspur into unusual activity, sweet and colourful. We hovered around its encampment like flies around jaggery in grocer Nathu's shop.

What transpired inside was always a mystery to us. Our elders did not take us to those shows. Nor were we allowed to go unescorted. If we ever insisted on accompanying them, they turned round and angrily reminded us that, 'Sons and daughters of gentle folk do not go to these exhibitions of vulgarity.' Sometimes they said: 'When you grow up and begin understanding the facts of life, then you may go and see such performances. But not now, you mealy-mouthed kids.'

If we persisted we were scolded, spanked and shut up. Our parents firmly believed that if we ever happened to see a film show or a theatrical performance, we would go astray from the narrow, straight path of virtue and miss the purpose of life. Any return to correct life would then be as impossible as caressing the sky.

Whether this was the truth and nothing but the truth our infantile reasoning could not figure out fully. But a film or a theatrical performance always remained an unextinguished craving. How to satisfy it was a problem forcing us to all manner of scheming.

At school, teachers dinned into our ears the glory of unquestioned obedience to parents; to hurt the feelings of parents even unwittingly or to fail to respect their wishes, even whims, was the depth of degradation. In the tussle between craving and duty we found the former was always stronger.

Some sort of a show was permitted to us only during the Dussehra holidays. The triangular drama of man, beauty and the devil represented by Rama, Sita and Ravana, respectively, was a great concession to us.

I was in the sixth or seventh standard when a theatrical company again strayed into Gurdaspur. I conspired with my younger brothers to persuade — force would, in fact, be the right word — father to take us to a show. We thought up a line of action and mugged up a few decisive sentences to waft our request to the heart of the man in father.

Our excitement grew with the decline of the day. Before the evening set in, we took our stand at the entrance, anxiously awaiting father's arrival. We sighted *Pitaji* at last; he came home with a stick in hand and in a grave mood. We respectfully made way for him. Noticing our unusual behaviour, he gave us a faint smile of approbation.

Heartened, we followed him into the house. On the way I winked to my younger brother. Now was the moment to open the issue. *Pitaji* was in an amicable mood. My brother answered in sign language: 'Don't think I am a coward or that I have forgotten. Let *Pitaji* change and have his glass of *sakanjbeen*.'

As usual father put the stick in corner, sat down upon a charpoy, called our younger brother, Billoo, and began fondling him. The opportunity was not lost on him. Haltingly, he farmed the request: *'Pitaji,* take us to the theatre tonight.'

Hari, the younger brother, immediately lent support in perfect rehearsed words.

Father's immediate reaction was to wave off that very serious proposition. But when he found us insistent, he said angrily: *'Ankh ka jadoo'* (Magic of the eyes) is not meant for you. You are kids.'

'But we must see it.' I insisted with obvious vehemence. Hardly had I finished the sentence when a slap descended on my cheek. Sobbing, I made for the door. My brothers followed humbled and humiliated.

This incident broke our spirits immediately. For days we were afraid to show up in father's presence. But all the time our teacher's other exhortation continued to echo in our ears: 'Man does not give up his efforts because of defeats and diffculties: failures are stepping stones to success.'

After the lapse of a week or so, the theatrical company announced its next play, the *'Mahabharata.'* I called my brothers to a conference. We discussed the issue and unanimously decided to press our demand again, but this time first on mother.

We filed gingerly into her room. She smiled and asked, 'Now whom is the army going to attack?'

We told her what we were after. Solemnly, she chanted father's oft-repeated sermon. But finding us adamant, she thundered and threatened. We remained unimpressed and went on repeating: 'Mataji, the Mahabarata is a religious play. You yourself often narrate stories from the epic. Why don't you take us to the play?'

Cornered, she said: 'Go and tell your father. He is after all the master of the house, not I?'

When father returned home in the evening, we put up our demand to him. He fretted and fumed, thundered and threatened and otherwise tried his utmost to wriggle out somehow. But the play was religious. Our demand could not be brushed aside.

That night father took us to the show. We were bursting with joy. This was our first victory.

We went into the theatrical hall — an improvisation for the occasion. Excitedly, we waited for the show to begin.

With the deafening explosion of a cracker, the curtain began rolling up — too slowly, we felt.

And nothing was visible on the stage: a thick wall of smoke stood between us and the stage. After the smoke dispersed we spotted out some male and female figures offering prayers in unison. The ritual over, the show began with one or two skits.

I was yawning and soon dozed off. I don't know how long I remained unawake. I was rudely woken up by father. With clenched teeth and suppressed anger, he was saying: 'You damned son of a sin! You son of a pig! I have had to spend hard-earned money only to see you go to sleep in the hall. Never ask me to take you anywhere again or you will regret it, I tell you.'

Jabbering, I woke up. I myself could not make out why I had dozed off.

I rubbed my eyes and looked at the stage. The Pandavas were locked in a gambling bout with their cousins, the Kauravas. With every throw of the dice, excitement rose in the hall. After losing all their worldly possessions, the Pandavas staked their common wife, Draupadi. Everyone was engrossed in the scene. I was pitying poor Draupadi and saying to myself: 'If I were the Pandavas I would never stake Draupadi for the life of me.'

No sooner had the Pandavas lost Draupadi than Duryodhana, the Kaurava chief, ordered that she should be brought in. She was dragged to the stage as a slave. When she tried to rush out she was forced back again by her hair by Dushasana, Duryodhana's mighty brother; she was made to sit in Duryodhana's lap.

After these insults, Duryodhana ordered Dushasana to strip her.

Everyone in the hall craned his neck and fixed his anxious gaze on the stage. The God-fearing among the audience began chanting, 'Ram Ram.'

When Dushasana began pulling off her *sari*, Draupadi closed her eyes, and with folded hands prayed for intervention by Lord Krishna, her brother: 'Have pity on me. Come to my rescue and save me from this dishonour. You have saved the honour of millions. Save mine too.'

Her prayers were touching.

When half of her *sari* had been pulled off, excitement mounted to a crescendo in the audience. Lord Krishna had thrown no wrap from the sky to cover Draupadi's shame.

Spectators started shouting: 'Cast the wrap, cast the wrap.'

The more enthusiastic among them could not rest content with shouts. They stood up and began yelling for the wrap, gesticulating angrily. Youngsters climbed up the chairs and benches and began whistling, howling and thumping.

With a heavy thud, a bench broke down and the clamour was stilled momentarily, bringing audience and players to familiar dimensions.

In that pin-drop silence a voice confided from somewhere behind the curtains and drapery: 'Lord Krishna won't throw down the wrap tonight; his salary has been in arrears for the last four months.'

tai eesree

Krishen Chander

I was in my final year at the Grant Medical College, in Calcutta and had come to Lahore for a few days to attend my elder brother's wedding which was to take place in our ancestral home in Kucha Thakar Das close to Shahi Mohalla. It was there that I first met *tai* Eesree.

Tai Eesree was not really my aunt; but she was the sort of person who made everyone want to call her *tai* — elder aunt. When her tonga came into our locality and someone shouted, 'There's *tai* Eesree!' a crowd of people, both old and young, men as well as women, ran up to receive her. Some helped her alight from her tonga.

Tai Eesree was an asthmatic and the slightest movement or speech, or even the sight of people left her out of breath. Some relatives produced money from their pockets to pay the tonga*wala*, but *tai* Eesree gave a wheezing cackle and told them that she had already paid. The way she spoke, struggling for breath, and her asthmatic laughter, was most attractive to me. The relatives looked crestfallen. They put their money back in their pockets and complained, 'Why did you do that? You don't give us an opportunity to do anything for you.' *Tai* did not answer. She took a fan from the hand of a young girl standing beside her and came along smiling and fanning herself.

Tai Eesree could not have been a day under sixty. Most of her hair had gone grey, making a pleasing frame for her brown, oval face. Everyone liked to hear her simple words, spoken through her asthmatic wheeze, but what fascinated me were her eyes. There was something about them which made me think of Mother Earth — of vast stretches of farmland and of deep flowing rivers — and at the same time they were full of boundless love and compassion, of fathomless innocence, and of sorrow unassuageable. To this day I have not met a woman with such eyes. They had that quality of timelessness which makes the biggest and the most difficult human problem appear insignificant.

Tai Eesree wore a *gharara* of taffeta with a gold border; her shirt was of saffron silk embroidered with flowers. And her head was covered with a muslin *duppatta*. She wore gold bracelets on her arms. As she came into the courtyard there was a great commotion. Young brides and aunts, brothers' wives and their sisters-in-law, mother's sisters and father's brother's wives all ran up to touch her feet. A woman fetched a multi-coloured *peerhi, tai* Eesree smiled and sat down on it. She embraced all the women in turn, put her hand on their heads and blessed them.

And beside them a young girl, Savitri began to wave a hand-fan with great enthusiasm. *Tai* Eesree had brought a coloured wicker basket with her, it lay beside her feet by the *peerhi*. As she blessed each person she took out a four-*anna pice* from the basket and gave one to everybody in turn. She must have given away over a hundred four-*anna pices* in twenty minutes. When all the men and the women, boys, girls, infants had touched her feet and received their four *anna pice, tai* Eesree raised her chin and turned back to look at the girl fanning her. 'Which one are you?' she asked.

'I am Savitri,' replied the girl shyly.

'*Ai hai,* you are Jai Kishen's daughter! I had completely forgotten you. Come and embrace me...'

Tai Eesree took the girl in her arms and kissed her face. By the time she had opened the basket and given the girl a four-*anna pice,* all the women were in fits of laughter. Aunt Kartaro flashed her sapphire ring and explained, '*Tai,* this Savitri is not Jai Kishen's daughter; she is the daughter of the untouchable Heero.'

'*Hai,* I am ruined!' wailed *tai* Eesree. She could hardly breathe. '*Hai,* I will have to wash myself thoroughly. I even kissed her on the face. What am I to do?'

Tai Eesree turned her bewildered eyes on the untouchable Savitri. The girl began to sob. This made *tai* relent at once. She took the girl in her arms again. 'No, child, you mustn't cry! You are quite innocent; you are as pure as a goddess, a virgin goddess. God Himself lives in your undefiled little body. You should not cry. I have to wash because my religion says I must. No more tears. Here's another four *annas* for you...'

Tai Eesree gave the girl a second four-*anna pice,* and the untouchable Savitri wiped her tears and began to smile. *Tai* Eesree then raised her arm to beckon. 'Heeroo! Warm water for my bath. You too will get four *annas.*' The crowd in the courtyard was convulsed with laughter.

Many people called *Tai* Eesree the four-*anna* aunty; others called her the sponsor aunty. It was well-known that from the day elder uncle Bodh Raj had married *tai* Eesree to the present time, their marriage had not been consummated. Scandalmongers even said that before his marriage, young Bodh Raj had so many affairs with beautiful, sophisticated women that when he found himself wedded to a simple peasant-girl he took an instant dislike to her and left her strictly alone. He did not maltreat her in any way; he sent her Rs. 75 every month; and she lived with her in-laws in the village and served everyone who came. Uncle Bodh Raj had an iron-monger's business in Jullundur and often it was many years before he went to his village. Eesree's parents tried several times to persuade her to come home, but she refused. Her parents even wanted to arrange another marriage of her, but *tai* would not hear of it. She looked after her husband's parents so well that they began to cherish her more than they could have their own daughter. Uncle Bodh Raj's father, Malik Chand handed over all the keys of the house to *tai* Eesree. Her mother-in-law became so fond of her that she gave away all her gold ornaments to *tai* Eesree.

About other stout women in general one may be justified in wondering how they cope with the problems of their youth, but no one had any doubts about *tai* Eesree. One was sure that even on the day she was born, she must have raised her hand to bless her own mother and spoken to her in her sweet compassionate voice — 'You have had to suffer much for my sake; here's a four *anna* bit for you!'

It was probably her temperament which made her relationship with her husband so peaceful. As far as their relatives were concerned, Uncle Bodh Raj was a good-for-nothing *bon-viveur* drunkard and fornicator. What if he had made good in his iron business! He had no right to ruin the life of *tai* Eesree the way he had. But *tai* Eesree herself had no regret whatsoever at having wasted her life; from the way she spoke and behaved it did not seem as if she were even aware of the fact that someone had ruined her life. She was always chatting merrily, laughing, joining people in their fun; always sharing people's joys and sorrows, always ready to lend a hand. It was inevitable that if there was a celebration in the neighbourhood, *tai* Eesree would be there. And if someone was bereaved, *tai* Eesree was there too, to share their grief.

Tai Eesree's husband had money, but not *tai* Eesree. The 75 rupees she received every month she invariably spent on other people. In those days money went a long way. The 75 rupees helped a lot of people in distress. But it wasn't *tai* Eesree's generosity that drew people to her. There were times when *tai* Eesree did not have a *pice* in her pocket and yet people flocked to her. On the contrary one often heard it said that merely to touch *tai* Eesree's feet, gave one peace of mind.

Uncle Bodh Raj was as satanic a man as *tai* Eesree was saintly. For thirty years he left *tai* Eesree to live with his parents in the village. When they died and the other members of the family had grown up, married and set up homes of their own, the house in the village was empty. Bodh Raj had no choice but to take *tai* Eesree to Jullundur. But *tai* Eesree was not able to stay there for more than a few days, because Bodh Raj attempted a liaison with the daughter of a respectable Pathan family from Pacca Bagh. The Pathans told *tai* Eesree that it was out of regard for her that they had spared the life of Bodh Raj and it would be best if she took her husband elsewhere. A few days later *tai* Eesree accompanied her husband to Lahore and rented a small house in Mohalla Varyaran. As luck would have it, even in Lahore Uncle Bodh Raj's business flourished. And at the same time he began to visit a prostitute Lachmi, who carried on her trade in Shahi Mohalla. The affair developed and finally Uncle Bodh Raj began to live with the whore, and seldom set foot in Mohalla Varyaran. But there was no trace of resentment in *tai* Eesree's face.

It was at the time when there was much talk of Uncle Bodh Raj's affair with the prostitute, when my elder brother's marriage took place. Bodh Raj did not come to the wedding but *tai* Eesree spent all her days and nights looking after the comforts of the guests. Her amiable ways smoothed the most uneven of tempers; scowls on people's faces turned to smiles.

I never heard *tai* Eesree criticise anyone, complain against fate, or seem out of her depth. Only once did I see in her a temporary disquiet.

This was during the wedding festivities. My elder brother was occupied all night with the wedding ceremonies. Early morning after the ceremony was over, the bride's people spread out the dowry for display. Those were old times when people gave coloured *peerhies* rather than the now fashionable sofa-sets; and beds with gaudily painted legs. Those were times when drawing rooms were known by their native names as *baithaks* or *diwan khanas*. But my elder brother's father-in-law was an executive officer in a Military cantonment; and the first Indian to have attained this rank. Consequently he gave his daughter a handsome dowry — all of it in the very latest style. Amongst our relatives this was the first time that anyone had given a sofa-set in a dowry.

The sofa-set was the main topic of conversation amongst our kinsmen. Women from distant localities came to the house to see the 'English *peerhoo*'. This was also the first time that *tai* Eesree saw a sofa-set. She examined it with great care; then she felt it with her hands and kept mumbling to herself. Unable to contain herself she turned to me for an explanation.

'Son, why is this thing called a sofa-set?'

How could I answer a question like that? I just shook my head — 'I have no idea aunty.'

'Why are the two chairs small and the third one long?' Again I did not know the answer and again shook my head to convey my ignorance.

Tai pondered over the matter for quite some time, clearly perplexed. Suddenly her face lit up with a childish radiance as if she had found the answer. 'Shall I tell you?'

'Yes, aunty.'

She explained to us as if we were a bunch of little children. 'Listen! I think the long sofa is meant for the time when the husband and wife are at peace with each other; then they can both sit on it. And whenever they have a quarrel they can sit separately on the two smaller ones. The English are a very wise race. No wonder they rule over us.'

Tai's reasoning aroused a roar of laughter. But I noticed that *tai* herself was suddenly silent. Was she reminded of the life-long misunderstanding between her own husband and herself? I could not say for certain. But when I looked up at her, I caught a strange light in her eye, as if somewhere a door in her mind always kept firmly locked, had opened for an instant.

After taking my medical degree from Calcutta, I married a Bengali girl and set up as a doctor in Dharamtola. I tried hard for several years but could not build up a practice. Eventually my elder brother persuaded me to move to Lahore. He set me up in a shop in Kucha Thakar Das and I started my practice amongst my own kinsmen and neighbours. At Calcutta I had been a young novice without any experience; at Lahore I started with almost ten year's know-how of the art of trapping patients. Consequently I did quite well. I was kept busy at all hours of the day and night.

I had my own family by now, so life went round in a whirl, with no time to go anywhere.

I did not see *tai* Eesree for many years. But I had heard that she still lived in the same house in Mohalla Varyaran and that Uncle Bodh Raj lived in Shahi Mohalla with his prostitute mistress, Lachmi. And that, once in a while he dropped in, to find out how his wife was faring.

One morning when I was making out prescriptions for the crowd of patients in my clinic, a man from Mohalla Varyaran came along and said — 'Doctor Sahib, *tai* Eesree is dying. Come along at once.'

I lelt my patients and went with the man. *Tai's* house was at the extreme end of Mohalla Varyaran. Climbing the flight of stairs I entered a dimly-lit room. *Tai* was reclining on her large pillows, breathing heavily. She was clutching her bosom with her right hand as if to keep her heart in its place. When she saw me, she smiled with relief. 'Son, now that you've come, I will be saved.'

'What's the trouble, aunty?'

'A call from the angel of death! I have had high fever for two days and then suddenly my body went cold (*Tai's* eye-lids fluttered as she spoke). First, life went out of my legs; when I touched them they were icy cold; if I pinched them, I felt nothing. Then slowly life went out of my belly. And when it was about to depart from the rest of my body, I clutched at my kidney. (*Tai* emphasized this by clutching her heart with greater vigour) — So I grabbed at my kidney and yelled, "Is anyone there? Go and fetch Jai Kishen's son Radha Kishen. He's the only one who can cure me!" Now you are here — now I know I will live,' she said with absolute conviction.

I stretched out my hand towards *tai's* right arm. 'Give me your arm; I will feel your pulse.'

She brushed away my hand with her left hand — '*Hai*, what kind of doctor are you!' she exclaimed. 'You don't even know that I am holding my life with this hand. How can I let you feel the pulse in this arm?'

In a few weeks *tai* was on her feet again. She had high blood pressure. When the pressure went down, she was able to walk about and resume her interest in the joys and sorrows of friends and strangers. Some months after she had got well, Uncle Bodh Raj passed away. He died of heart-failure in the house of his mistress.

Tai did not allow his body to be brought to her house. His bier was taken from Shahi Mohalla. She would not accompany the cortege nor go to the cremation ground. Not a tear came to her eye. Without saying a word she broke up her marriage bangles, changed from her coloured garments into a plain white dhoti, rubbed away the vermillion powder in the parting of her hair and smeared a little ash on her forehead. That was all she did to conform to religious tradition.

The plain white suited her grey hair and she looked comelier than before. There was some gossip amongst the relatives about the strange behaviour of *tai* Eesree. Everyone was a little surprised; some were even pained. But so great was their respect for *tai* Eesree that no one could dare to say anything to her.

The years went by. My practice now extended beyond Mohalla Thakur Das to Kucha Karmal inside Shahalmi Gate up to the main square in Wachhowali. In the mornings I was at Mohalla Thakur Das and the evenings in Wachhowali. The days were spent in work and at times I was not able to see *tai* Eesree for a year or more. Nevertheless I got all her news from the women of the family. Uncle Bodh Raj had left all he had in the bank to Lachmi, but had willed a house and a shop in Jullundur to *tai* Eesree. This gave *tai* Eesree a rent of 150 rupees every month. She continued to live in Mohalla Varyaran as busy as before in her rituals and charities.

One day after seeing a patient I happened to be passing through Shahi Mohalla. I suddenly thought of Uncle Bodh Raj and then of Lachmi who lived in Shahi Mohalla and from Lachmi my thoughts travelled to *tai* Eesree. I had a pang of conscience as, I had not been to see her for over twelve or fifteen months. I resolved to call on her at the first oppurtunity in the next day or two.

100

I was still sunk in thought when I saw *tai* Eesree come out of a lane in the Mohalla. Instead of her usual *gharara* she was wearing a black one without any hem or ruffles. Even her *kameez* was a plain white one and she had a white muslin *duppatta* which she had wrapped round her head and chin making her look exactly like an early madonna.

She saw me almost as soon as I saw her. And she suddenly seemed very embarrassed and turned back into the lane from which she was coming. I called out to her. My voice had a note of alarm in it. What was *tai* Eesree doing in the prostitutes' quarter?

'*Tai* Eesree!' I cried '*Tai* Eesree!'

She heard me and turned, facing me, head down, like a criminal pleading his guilt.

'*Tai* Eesree, what are you doing here?' I asked in surprise and anger.

She could not meet my eyes. 'Son,' she said, in a faltering tone, 'What can I say? except that... that... I heard that that Lachmi woman was not well... very sick... so I thought perhaps I should go and see her...'

'You came here to see Lachmi' I screamed at her — 'Lachmi that sluttish whore, the bitch that...'

Tai Eesree raised her hand, and silenced me — '*Na, na*, son' she said gently. 'Don't say anything against her.' She raised her eyes and breathed a long sigh. 'She was the only thing left by which I could remember my late husband. Today even that remembrance is gone.'

When the riots flared up in 1947 we left Lahore and came to Jullundur because *tai* Eesree had a house there. She gave the top-floor for herself. Everyday she went to the refugee camp and gave whatever help she could. Sometimes she would return home with an orphan or two. In four or five months she had four boys and three girls living with her, because no trace could be found of their parents. She also let refugees use her courtyard and the yard at the back of the house.

In a short while her house began to look like a caravanserai. Nevertheless, not once did an angry frown darken *tai* Eesree's brow. She entered her own house as if she were a stranger and had been allowed in by the refugees to whom it belonged. Women have an obsession for personal possessions. But I have never met even a man — far less a woman — who had as little use for possessions. Perhaps nature had left a vacuum in that part of the head which longs for property. Whatever she owned was in trust for other people. When she came to Jullundur she began to eat only one meal a day, but she never complained.

I was tense and easily irritated in those days and *tai* Eesree's simple acceptance often annoyed me. I had lost a lucrative practice in Lahore and my house in Model Town had been left behind. And now I did not have a roof over my head — no clothes, nor money, not even enough for a square meal. We ate what we were given, when it was given, and if it wasn't given, we went hungry. And during these days I was stricken with dysentery. Being a doctor myself I tried all the medicines I knew. But with an affliction like this one, one needs very careful dieting. How could I arrange that? My health deteriorated rapidly. For sometime I was able to conceal this from *tai*, but then she found out about it. She came to my room and spoke most anxiously: 'Son, you take my advice, this is dysentery. Doctors know nothing about it. What you must do — and I'll give you the fare — is to go straight to Gujranwala. In the goldsmiths' lane lives Uncle Karim Bux, the barber. He has a wonderful medicine which can cure the worst type of dysentery. Your uncle had the same trouble about 20 years ago; it was uncle Karim Bux who rid him of it. He spent ten days in Gujranwala and came back to Jullundur absolutely fit and healthy.'

I flared up. 'For heaven's sake, *tai*, don't you know I cannot go to Gujranwala?'

'Why not? I'll give you money for the fare.'

'Money is not the problem. Gujranwala is in Pakistan.' 'So what? Can't we go there to get medicine. Our uncle Karim Bux...'

'*Tai*, you know nothing,' said I interrupting her irritably. 'You go on making the most naive suggestions. The Muslims have now made a separate country for themselves; it is called Pakistan. Our country is known as Hindustan. No Hindustanis can go to Pakistan now, nor Pakistanis come to Hindustan. They have to have passports.'

Tai's forehead wrinkled in consternation. 'Passcourt? Do you have to go to court for it?'

'Yes, of course.' I replied in exasperation, to end the argument. It was too much bother to explain the details to the old crone.

'No son, it's not nice to go to court. Sons of respectable families never go to the courts. But our uncle Karim Bux...'

'Karim Bux be damned!' I yelled at the top of my voice. 'You talk of twenty years ago: You don't even know if your uncle Karim Bux is alive or dead, but you go on repeating his name like a parrot.'

Tai turned away with tears in her eyes. After she had gone I felt stricken with remorse for my quick temper. Why had I hurt the simple, guileless woman? If *tai* was unable to grasp the complications of present day life, what fault was it of hers?

It was a time of frayed nerves and tempers. At college I had always talked of revolution. Later, when I prospered in life and my practice flourished, the ardour for revolution was somewhat cooled; in due course the word itself vanished from my vocabulary. The difficult days at Jullundur revived my zeal for the revolution. I sought the company of likeminded people who too had nothing more to lose; we would foregather and discuss the revolution with great enthusiasm. The meetings were usually in my room, on the second floor of *tai* Eesree's house. We would have many rounds of tea and discuss the problems of the world. I, working myself into a frenzy would wave a clenched fist and shout, 'We are not being treated fairly. We should not expect any justice from these people. I am convinced there will be another *inqilab* (revolution) in this country and it must come soon.'

Tai Eesree overheard us one day. She came in, extremely worried and asked, 'Son, are the Muslims coming?'

'No aunty! who told you so?'

'Who is this *inqilab* you said was on his way here?'

Poor *tai*, she believed *inqilab* was the name of some Muslim. When we grasped what she was thinking, we went into fits of laughter.

'How simple you are *tai*! Dear, aunty we are talking about an *inqilab* which is neither Hindu or Muslim. It belongs to all; we want to bring it here.'

It was too much for *tai*, she shook her head and gave up. 'All right, you boys go on with your discussion. I will bring you some tea.

To help me out of my predicament, *tai* sold her gold bracelet. With the money I was able to take my family to Delhi, as

Jullundur was still very unsettled and had a depressing atmosphere. I set up my practice anew in Delhi and in a few years I was on my feet again. My clinic was in Karol Bagh where a large number of refugees from Lahore had settled. Many knew me. Slowly but surely I got them to come to me and began to make a handsome income. In ten years I was able to build a house for myself and buy a car. I became the leading citizen of Karol Bagh. Once again I gave up the talk of revolution. The dysentery left me. So did the irritability. I became as amiable as a good doctor should be.

After thirteen years I had occasion to return to Jullundur last March, to attend the wedding of a relative. In these thirteen years I had all but forgotten the existence of *tai* Eesree. One can make time for relations only when one has no patients. However, as soon as I got to Jullundur, my thoughts returned to her and all she had done for me; particularly the gold bangle which had helped me to resume my practice. I had never paid back the money. From Jullundur railway station I went straight to *tai* Eesree's house.

It was dusk. The air was laden with dust and smoke and the smell of oil. The voice of children returning to their homes filled the evening as I entered *tai* Eesree's house.

There was no one in the house besides *tai* Eesree, her head bowed in prayer. She had lit an oil lamp and was offering flowers to her god. At the sound of my footsteps she stepped back and called, 'Who is it?'

'It is I,' I answered, entering and smiling at her.

Tai came up another two paces but was unable to recognise me. Thirteen years is a long time! She had become somewhat deaf and her eyes were weak. Her face looked thinner than before and she walked very slowly.

'I am Radha Kishen,' I said softly.

'Jai Kishen's little boy?' *tai's* voice was full of emotion. Fearing she might hasten her step and lose her balance, I went up to her quickly and held her. She clung to me and began to cry. She blessed me a hundred times, kissed my face, patted me on the head, murmuring, 'Son, where were you all these days? Where have you been? It's been so long!'

I felt thoroughly ashamed of myself and lowered my head. I tried to speak but the words would not come. *Tai* understood my embarrassment and changed the subject, asking, with her old asthmatic wheeze, 'Is Saroj well and happy?'

'Yes *tai.*'

'And the elder boy?'

'He is studying medicine.'

'And the younger?'

'He is in college.'

'And Shanno and Banto?'

'Both the girls are in college. I got Kamla married.'

'Good, good!' she nodded her head in satisfaction. 'I also got Savitri married off,' she said. 'Pooran is at Roorki. Nimmi and Bumy found their parents. They took them away after six years of separation! Wasn't that wonderful? I still hear from them from time to time. Only Gopi is left with me now. Next year he too will leave me, to work as an apprentice at the railway workshop.'

This was an account of the orphans that *tai* had adopted during the riots.

I scratched my chin sheepishly and said, '*Tai,* I haven't yet paid the debt I owe you. I am thoroughly ashamed of myself for not having sent the money. I will send it to you as soon as I get back to Delhi.'

'What kind of debt?' asked *tai* very surprised.

'You remember, the bracelet?'

'Oh that!' It came back to her and she smiled very softly. She stroked my head and said, 'That was in payment of the debt I owed you.'

'You did not owe me anything, *tai!*' I exclaimed.

'Son, this life itself is a debt we owe other people,' said *tai* in a grave voice. 'One should always keep repaying parts of it. Did you come into this world on your own? No, your parents gave you life. Don't you then owe the debt of your life to someone else? If we did not repay this debt, how would the world progress? The day of reckoning will come... Son, that is why I say I paid the debt I owed you. You must pay the debt you owe to someone else. Always redeem your debt — that should be the law of life.' So long a sermon left *tai* completely out of breath.

What could I say to her? What can the shadow say to the light? I heard what she had to say and kept my silence. She too was silent for a while and then she spoke again, 'Neither my hands nor my feet are any good now; otherwise I'd have cooked a meal for you. When Gopi comes back, he will make something for you. You mustn't leave before I have given you something to eat... yes?'

I said humbly, '*Tai* please don't bother about it now. Everything we eat today is because of you.' I spoke slowly, 'I came to attend Tej Pal's wedding. From the railway station I came straight to your house, but I must now join the wedding party.'

'Ah yes,' she said. 'I too was invited. But I have been feeling out of sorts for the last two days and have decided not to go. I have sent them a present. You pat Tej Pal on the head on my behalf and give him my blessings.'

'Most certainly, aunty,' I said, bending down to touch her feet. She clasped me to her bosom. With her hand on my head, she blessed me a hundred times. 'Son,' she said suddenly as I turned to go, 'can you do something for me?'

'You only have to say it.'

'Please come and see me tomorrow morning?'

'Why, aunty,' I laughed, 'What's the matter? I've only just seen you now!'

Tai spoke haltingly. 'My eyesight is very bad; at night I cannot see at all. If you were to come sometime in the daytime I could have a good look at you. I haven't seen you for thirteen years, son.'

My eyes filled with tears. I replied — 'I will certainly come, aunty.'

Next morning more wedding guests were due to arrive and a few of us went to the railway station to receive them. On our way back, I recalled my promise, asked my companions to excuse me and went towards *tai* Eesree's house. Around the corner of the lane on which she lived, there were little groups of people standing with their heads lowered. I ignored them and quickened my pace. On the ground floor of her house many others were gathered, all of them in tears. *Tai* Eesree had died that morning, while I was at the railway station.

They had laid her on the floor of her room wrapped in a white sheet. Her face was uncovered. There was an odour of burning camphor and incense. A *pandit* was chanting Vedic *mantras*.

Tai Eesree's eyes were shut, her child-like face already grey. It had something of an eternal loneliness in it, a peace, a dissolution in fathomless dreams which made it look, not like the face of the *tai* Eesree that I had known, but of the vast earth itself — the earth in whose eyes ran the rivers of the world, in whose lap were a hundred thousand valleys where human habitations were sheltered by smiling mountains; mountains, from which rose the fragrance of selfless love and the radiance of innocence.

I was standing at her feet gazing on her face when someone put a right hand on my shoulder. I turned round and saw a young man. His eyes were swollen with weeping.

'I am Gopi Nath,' he said softly.

I realised who he was but made no comment. I did not know what to say.

'I went to look for you in Tej Pal's house; you had left for the railway station.'

I remained silent.

'*Tai* asked for you several times this morning. She knew you would come to see her. She waited for you till her last breath. When she knew she could wait no longer, she said to me —- "When my son Radha Kishen comes, give him this."'

Gopi Nath stretched out his hand and placed a four *anna pice* in the flat of my palm.

I broke down and cried.

I do not know where *tai* Eesree is today, but if she is in heaven I am certain that even now she is sitting on her coloured *peerhi*, with her open wicker basket at her feet, patting the heads of the gods and giving them each a four *anna pice*.

the blind alley

Gurmukh Singh Jeet

Despite numerous efforts, inder could not shake off the effects of yesterday's happenings. So far he had been spared worries in his life, but the very first impact had sent him off the rails. The more he tried to forget the unfortunate incident, the deeper grew the furrows left by it on his mind.

Although he was not fond of seeing films very often, he thought that seeing one today might divert his mind and soothe him, so after his dinner he said to his youngest daughter, 'Nirmal, tell your mother that I shall return late in the night.' And quietly he set out of his house. In his ears the words of the Superintendent were resounding still: 'Inder, if you want to continue in service, you must be very careful. I don't require good-for-nothing fellows like you, I tell you!'

'Good-for-nothing! Good-for-nothing! Am I really so?' he kept wondering.

Only a few days ago, after the accounts of the company were audited, his Superintendent had been all praise for his work, which was indeed flawless. And yet what did he say yesterday? Oh! How strange these people are! And fickle in their opinions! At one time they hold one opinion and at another time quite a different one. It takes them no time to change their minds, weather-cocks! Whosoever works strenuously, slaving ten hours instead of the official eight, is a Yes-man like I am, Inder thought. Such a slave takes scoldings from his boss; never asks for an increment or for an enhancement of his dearness allowance, even though his children are starving and often he himself has to attend office on an empty stomach. Yet these are the men who are regarded as worthy and patted on the back like dogs. A strange standard indeed!

Walking slowly in a gloom, Inder reached the picture house. Today neither the flying end of a gold-bordered sari nor a colourful blouse could attract his attention. He was completely lost in himself.

The house was full, packed to capacity. Although his eyes were fixed on the screen, his heart was sunk in abysmal depths. While people followed the story with rapt attention, his mind was wandering elsewhere. The colourful scenery, the popular music and the young heroine in the picture, all failed to stir his emotions. Inder sat through the picture brooding. So absorbed was he in his own thoughts that he was unaware for a few minutes that the show was over. When he came to himself, he staggered home at midnight. His heart was heavy as before.

The lamp was fluttering hazily. His wife, tired of waiting, had fallen half-asleep in a chair. Her eyelids drooped with drowsiness but her ears were alert for the opening of the door. Her dishevelled dark hair could not conceal the fine molding and delicacy of her features. He watched her for a while from the window, framed in the faint light, small, fragile, in her green poplin. Shakuntla was one of those women whose ideal is to serve their husbands at all costs and in all circumstances. Hearing his step, she rose readily to open the door. He walked in and threw himself on his bed without uttering a word. But unable to sleep, he tossed restlessly.

Time and again he relived the day and was convinced of his own innocence. The matter for which he was scolded yesterday, was not his fault, he thought. Even a healthy, well-fed man, working from 9 in the morning till 7 or 8 in the evening in the heat of summer, might get confused. How much more reason for a man like himself, who never even saw a cup of milk except on those rare occasions when it was served to his children. Butter, he could only think of as an ingredient of offerings to gods.

He always worked very hard, very conscientiously. But last evening, while totalling the account, his pencil had put the digit 7 instead of 9. It was really a slip of the pen and no blunder, yet that was precisely the reason for which he had had to swallow so much against his self-respect.

It was not a major error, either, especially when he would have corrected it the very next morning, while double-checking the accounts as usual. But misfortunes attended him. He did not get the opportunity. The Superintendent called for those very papers and his eye eventually fell on the mistake. The silly clerical slip which would not have occurred at all, had he not been in a particular hurry last evening to leave the office and take home medicine for his ailing child.

With such thoughts roving in his mind and a growing feeling of uneasiness, Inder was exhausted. Within him, a storm was raging. His breast heaved, as the earth heaves with lava before a volcano erupts. Within him clashed opposite currents of thought.

As the turmoil increased, he rose from his bed, then lay down and rose again. But feeling that many hours were left before day-break, he lay down again, his mind immersed in confusion.

He was helpless. The Superintendent's words had left a sting, but who was there to sympathise? Continuously he thought, 'They draw fat salaries for themselves, but for us it is always a fixed salary: Rs. 59 and As. 15. The employer is only concerned with multiplying his gross profits; little does he care for those who help him to run the business and accumulate wealth. Like the famous Shaikh Chillie, he cuts the very branch on which he is perching. Intoxicated with his wealth, the shrieks of a starving child, the groan of an ailing infant, the sight of a youth, torn with anxiety, fail to touch his heart. His riches and his houses are all built on the sweat and toil of down-trodden people like me. Cruel, stone-hearted, callous!

'If his heart is not moved at the sight of a sick child, is he fit to be called a human being? Surely not! He is a cannibal. He is unconcerned if someone is dying with cold outside his house, as long as he himself is wrapped in warm clothes, eating and drinking of the best. These haughty men!'

With such furious thoughts creating havoc in his mind, Inder trembled with anger.

His soul was not yet so degraded, he told himself, that he would own defeat in the first encounter. His sinews had still some of the energy of youth left in them.

Thus does the wick of a dying lamp burn brighter before it finally goes out. A new confidence flickered in his otherwise feeble physical frame. He was still mentally vigorous enough to clear his conscience, he decided, and he would not put up with this mean and unjust treatment. It was intolerable. For a moment he wavered indecisively between the prospects of starvation and of continuing in service, to swallow insults and humiliation. Then he chose starvation and all the consequences. The die was cast!

Yes, he would resign his job on the morrow.

After taking this fateful decision, he could no longer lie in bed. He resolved to write his resignation letter then and there. Rising he searched for a match box in the darkness. Sincere efforts rarely go in vain. His hand touched the box and he lit the lamp. But the light flickered and went out. The oil had run out! He found himself helpless against such odds.

Exhausted, he again groped his way back to his bed, staggering a little with weakness. He heard his child coughing in the other room; and all at once his thoughts took a new turn. Inder pondered anew his decision to resign! By resigning his job, was he not throwing his son into the jaws of death? Was he not leaving his wife to confront the battle of life? Was he not a deserter? Was he not preparing for himself the slippery path for his own fall into the bottomless abyss? Was not his resignation his own death warrant? Good heavens! he thought, he had been about to take a wrong step! He owed responsibility to his family, and he had been about to neglect it. For himself he could face starvation, but what of his wife and children? A cruel, callous society was unlikely to feed them, or to treat them with care. And the result would only be frightful and ignominious death! The thoughts of tragedy again gnawed at him.

'Daddy! Daddy! Get up! Even the sun is out. Hurry up and go to office,' cried his daughter Nimmi. She was voicing the words of her mother and knocking at the door of her father's bedchamber. In the morning sun he could see the tender eager face, with moist dark hair curling loosely at her temple.

Inder was startled. He was unaware that the whole night had passed. Rubbing his eyes with his palms, he climbed out of bed. On his face was only dejection and disappointment, no trace remained of his vigorous revolt. 'You are a family man Inder,' he said to himself, 'you have a devoted wife and children to look after!' From some inner reccess of his heart he heard a cry of despair, but he stifled it, stifled his self-respect, his hopes of proud action.

With a little whisper of submission, quickly he washed his face, proceeded to don his clothes and swallowed his breakfast. In a little while, taking his cycle, with a bundle of files tied on to the carrier, he was seen peddling along the road to his office. The day stretched ahead of him, lengthening, in his mind, into weeks, years, a lifetime. A long, dreary road and no way out.

Saadat

Yashpal

This has been my sitting-room for six years now. Its red floor is used to all sorts of footmarks, but it retains no trace of them to remind one of the people who have been in it. Still, just near the door leading into the house, two paws of a cat are imprinted for ever. They will last as long as the floor itself, because they were left there by a cat when the floor was being laid. Whenever I see these marks I cannot help thinking of incidents from my early childhood — that tender age when one acquires impressions that last a whole lifetime — when I hadn't even joined a primary school.

My father was an official in the Forests Division. At times he used to take us — that is mother and the children along with him on tours.

It was a hilly terrain. Our camps were pitched near a well on the roadside. Cars, trucks, horses, tongas and a perennial stream of pedestrians — in short, all the things that are associated with the idea of a road, were missing there. A comparatively broad ribbon of a footpath wound up hill and down dale. Occasionally *pahari* men and women passed in groups. Usually women carried small bundles balanced on their heads and men carried bundles on their backs. Another picture of that period well-preserved in my mind, is that of a man following his two or three mules, carrying a thick stick on his shoulder, and singing in a high voice, with a hand on his ear and his face upturned. This was all the crowd that the road was accustomed to.

I don't remember the number of days we lived there. But I had memorised many songs I frequently heard on the road and at the well. I have forgotten school and college lessons in History and Chemistry, but I can still recite a few haunting lines from those songs:

'Goriye da man lagya Chambe di ghati
Kunja jai paiyan nadaun,
Thandhe pani te banke nahon,
Pal bhar bahi lain, ho dayara.'

(The belle has fallen in love with the valley of Chamba
'The *kronch* birds alight on the Nadaun river;
The dandies bathe in its cool water;
O *devar,* let us sit here awhile.')

And on a slope near the well, the breeze played through thick pines and their needle leaves, in a sound that was half song, half sigh.

There was a grave beneath one of the trees, and nearby were two huts inhabited by some people. They had a pair of big, bear-like, black dogs and some hens. We — that is my younger sister and I — used to play with the dogs and the hens. Most of the time we were at the huts.

And of all these memories, the centre, the heart, is Saadat. Even after the passage of so much time and after so many revolutionary changes in my life, her figure is very distinct in my memory. She held her *duppatta* between her thumb and forefinger and touched the ground to *salaam* our mother. In our mother's presence she always sat on the bare ground — not like a sophisticated city girl. She sat with her feet outstretched and her knees played together ceaselessly. Her eyes, blue-grey, and her fine lips smiled always, setting aglow the peach-gold of her complexion and accentuating the proud line of a delicately chiselled nose.

She addressed Sita, my younger sister, as Munni. Sita too was very fond of her. Saadat lived with us in our camp. She talked to mother and helped her do odd jobs. But first and foremost she was a baby-sitter. She was there to look after Sita. Once with her, Sita forgot everyone else, even mother.

After that, during my childhood, I often heard mother telling her friends and acquaintances: 'I have seen beauty but once. Oh, she was a jewel in that rubbish heap.'

There is a saying that a woman is never charmed by another woman's beauty. But here a woman's beauty had charmed another. 'I have seen beauty but once,' mother would say, 'On the road from Kangra to Nadaun is the Tomb of Pir Chamola. There, in the family of the caretakers Saadat was a new bride. No queen ever dreamt of possessing beauty like hers. One glimpse of her could make one forget both hunger and thirst. And, oh, she was so sweet-tempered that neither of the children ever wanted to leave her...Yes even children can recognise beauty; even they sought her company...'

In my boyhood, stealthily, I often heard my mother say: 'Ah, if I could get such a beautiful bride for my son, I would pick her even off the dust.' And I would smile to hear her.

After that, whenever I read beauty described in stories and poems, or tried to imagine the beauty of Shakuntala or Zulekha, a clear image of the fair Saadat came to my mind. Whenever my parents talked of my marriage, I could not help remembering Saadat.

Perhaps they had forgotten all about Saadat, but to me she became more and more real every day. To me beauty meant Saadat. And at the same time I laughed at myself, because I

118

knew Saadat's beauty to be a thing of the past. I knew twenty long years must have snatched away her charms.

With a university degree and a doctorate, I got a job as a lecturer. I earned my living for the first time and felt manly, self-confident. Now I, myself, began to think of marriage. I dreamt of a home of my own, of my future wife and of our child. And then, I felt transported, eager to meet the future.

Well, that was all inevitable, I thought. It would come about as surely as the seasons return. Meanwhile I decided to visit a hill station in the summer vacation.

Something in my mind was always dragging me towards that shrine of Beauty, of which Saadat had been the only symbol for me, for so many years. But reason mocked at my heart. Would she be the same after twenty years? Wasn't it a hopeless quest? Is there a flower that doesn't wither? What can stay firm and unaltered under the fatal wheel of time? I knew and understood all this, yet it was there that I knew I would go.

I reached Kangra. There was a road now, leading from Kangra to Nadaun. Buses plied on it. I alighted from the bus at Ranital. The small lake on the shoulder of the hill, amidst cypress and pine trees, looked familiar, like a place seen in dreams.

I had no hope of seeing Saadat. But I was eager to see the place which had given me an ideal of beauty, where I came in contact with beauty unattachedly and for the first time in my life. Moreover I wanted to see the caretakers of Pir Chamola, who had had beauty incarnate live among them. The association of the idea had elevated beauty in my mind to a place higher than that of a mother; beauty, for me, had become something to be worshipped, revered and idolised; it was almost a faith with me.

I inquired my way up to the Tomb of Pir Chamola. Whispering pines on the mountain slope, red withered needles of pines strewn on the earth, lush verdure of turf underfoot, and mango groves below in the valley — all was like a familiar dream come true. The white-washed Tomb of Pir Chamola beneath a cluster of pines lay ahead. The huts of the caretakers stood behind the Tomb. Around me, the pines soared much higher than any I remembered in dreams.

I recognised the well at once. In fact it was a spring of fresh water, flowing down in a clear stream. The green scrub around the spring was thicker now, and shy violets grew in its shade. I thought, all is just as it was before, only I am not the same. And nor are the people who lived here once. Saadat will not be here and even if she were, she would be like the dry and scentless petals of a rose preserved only for the sake of happy memories. Why is human beauty so transitory?

Below, near the spring, sat an old man, wearing a blue loincloth. He had a small *hookah* under his armpit and nearby were two clay pitchers. Smoking his *hookah*, he filled a small vessel with water and emptied it into the pitchers.

I left the footpath to come down to the well. I wanted to speak to the caretaker, but before I could do so, he himself broke the silence.

I was startled. I could not believe my ears. The next moment the hermit called out again! 'Saadat, O S-a-a-d-a-t.' The sound echoed from the hills.

Now I will see Saadat, I thought. Saadat too must be like this old man, decayed and worn and tattered. They will pick up one pitcher each and take it home.

But she is still alive! She — the relic of beauty. The very fact of being able to see her again brought an upsurge of emotion, constricting my throat.

'I am coming, father.' In another moment the hills re-echoed the answer.

I raised my eyes in the direction from where the answer had come. I could not see anybody on the mound of the Tomb, but the thrill and youthfullness of the voice was unmistakable. The voice had the spring-time sweetness and the melody of a *koel's* song. Is this the voice of Saadat? I asked myself. Is Saadat a goddess of eternal beauty, like Menaka and Urvashi? Is she an imperishable image of the abstract idea of perfect youth?

Then a damsel came down a footpath from the mound of the Tomb, gliding with the effortless grace that is mountain-bred. She was wearing dark-blue and an empty pitcher was balanced on her head, upside down. I watched with delight the freedom and lightness of her movements.

The beauty of Saadat was before me, in flesh and blood. Pearly skin, wide blue-grey eyes, a fine-drawn nose and laughing lips. Exciting breasts, more exciting in the rhythm of her swinging gait. She looked towards me, full of curiosity, and then probably my eager and ardent stare made her shrink back and turn away.

She put her pitcher down lightly on the platform around the well. She whispered a few words to the old man. Then, smiling radiantly, she lifted the filled pitcher gently with both her hands. She threw another glance at me, and started climbing the hill, leaving me trembling with joyous excitement.

I moistened my dry tongue, and *salaamed* the old caretaker. 'I don't see much water in the spring today,' I casually remarked. Indeed, the quantity of the water flowing from the spring was very small and a pitcher could not be plunged in it.

The old man touched his forehead and replied, 'Yes, sir. We have to face this shortage almost daily during the summer.'

Now I thought it fit to remind him of our acquaintance of twenty years ago. He surveyed me from head to foot, with his rheumy eyes. 'Yes, indeed, sir,' he said at last, 'A Hindu who was an official in the Forests Division, camped here for about two months, twenty years ago. He was very kind.'

'My mother tells me of one Saadat *Bibi,* who lived here. She wanted me to *salaam* her on her behalf,' I tried to reinforce my failing courage.

'Yes, sir,' he answered calmly, 'She is the mother of this lass. She is very old and infirm now. Neither of us can carry a pitcher of water up the slope any more. This daughter of ours is a great help to us. She too is named Saadat.' Fondly he added, 'She looks just like her mother did when she was young!'

The young Saadat was gliding down the slope once more. On seeing me talking to her father, she lost her shyness and came up to the second pitcher. Ah, that lithe young form as it lifted the pitcher! An invisible arrow pierced my heart, leaving me mute and helpless, overwhelmed by her loveliness.

I went up to the hut with the old man, to see the first Saadat. When he told her who I was, the old woman caressed me with affection. She asked me numerous questions about my mother and reminisced gaily over my childhood in that summer long ago. The new Saadat watched me with wide, curious eyes, bashful when I met her glance. She offered me figs and strawberries and milk.

She sat opposite me, just as once her mother had sat opposite my mother, like a doe, innocent of fear of the hunter. Much as I wanted it, my eyes would not rest on her. Perhaps I had no courage to look at her as I longed to. For all the things that my mother used to wish for in her future daughter-in-law were echoing and re-echoing in my mind; and a knowledge of the impossibility of it all, of my own helplessness, was freezing my heart.

I had to return to Kangra by the afternoon bus. So I said my farewells and left. I walked back, downcast and miserable. I had gone there that day with no hope of seeing the beauty I had idolised for so many years. I had looked on it as a pilgrimage to a shrine. It was the unexpected reality that had disturbed my equilibrium. Beauty was no more a mere idol to worship; it was a tangible, living source of heartbreak and longing.

I have not been able to forget Saadat and her beauty, though the passionate longings are long since dead. I know now that the beauty of a woman is not mortal like her human form. It is something as eternal as truth itself.

Soorma singh

Balwant Singh

Where I was standing there was yet no rain; but I could hear it beat down on the corrugated-tin roofs of the houses on the hillside. It sounded almost like a procession of singers marching up towards me. It was apparent that in a few moments the rain would spread over the entire hill. Those familiar with this phenomenon could be seen hurrying towards places of shelter.

The sky was overcast and the damp in the air was like a wet sponge. I did not want to turn back. I looked up at the shelter where ponies were swishing their tails to keep away flies. The flies went from one pony to another and then settled on the face of their owner.

I quickened my pace. One could never tell with the rains in the hills! It could be pouring and a minute later the sun would break through. I could do worse than spend quarter of an hour in the pleasant company of a herd of pack-horses.

The gentle pitter-patter of the rain drops turned into a roar. People scurried in different directions; only those who had raincoats and hat covers were unconcerned. They had to get their money's worth! It was amongst this lot that I first espied Soorma Singh.

Soorma Singh had no raincoat, nor cover for his turban; he did not even have an umbrella. He had dark sun-glasses. He wore coarse hand-spun shirt, loose kneelength *kaccha* and a pair of Indian style slippers on his feet. His turban consisted of a couple of yards of plain white cloth wrapped untidily round the head; on his right wrist was a thick, steel bangle, the Sikh *kara*. He had a staff in his hand and was walking briskly along the road. He obviously wanted to escape the rain, but I concluded he was unwilling to share the company of hill ponies.

I was wrong. He walked alongside another person, placed his hand on the other's shoulder and said something to him. The other man took him by the hand and conducted him to the pony shed. It was then that I realised that Soorma Singh was blind.

Just as it is customary among Hindus to name blind men Soordas and among Muslims to call them Hafizjee, the Sikhs give their blind the name Soorma Singh.

Soorma Singh was still a few paces from the shed when the rain began to come down in a torrent. It did not drench Soorma Singh, but at places his shirt stuck to his body and rain drops glistened on his moustache and beard. The first thing he did was to take off his glasses and wipe the dark lenses with an enormous hankerchief. He put them back on his nose after carefully readjusting the shafts behind his ears. He stood with his staff, a few paces from me.

The man who had helped Soorma Singh to the shed turned back into the rain. His foot slipped and he fell heavily on his seat. A strange reward for a good turn! The man roared with laughter, rose with alacrity and proceeded on his way planting his feet more firmly on the ground.

Soorma Singh's mouth was half open; one of his canine teeth showed distinctly. It must have been a diseased tooth filled in by the dentist; the filling had gone and only a muddy cavity remained — somewhat like the hollow sockets of his eyes.

I stared at him as if he were a denizen from another world. Some instinct made him aware of my presence and he took an uncertain step in my direction. A pony neighed. Quickly he retraced his step — believing he had mistaken the pony for man.

I was staying in the local *gurdwara;* anyone can stay in a *gurdwara* for four days without paying anything. Thereafter, all that is necessary is to make an offering of a rupee to the Holy Book. That is good for a month. It even entitles one to a separate room. In this *gurdwara* most rooms had an attached kitchenette. On the ground-floor there were four bathrooms and latrines made of corrugated sheets: the stink pervaded the floors above. The living rooms were in the rear; the large prayer hall was on the top-floor — well beyond the foul odours of the latrines. The *gurdwara* gate opened on the metalled road. By the gate was a small free dispensary.

I was given a room on the middle floor without an attached kitchen. My servant, a boy from the hills, made my tea and cooked my meals on a stove in the room.

Although the *gurdwara* was in a congested locality, the adjoining houses did not crowd around it. Mule trains bringing loads from the plains were constantly passing in front of the *gurdwara.* It was only at 10 a.m. when the sweepers had cleaned the latrines and sprinkled phenyl that the place was free of smell; by then the mule caravans would reach the top of the hill. One could hear their copper bells from a distance. As they passed the *gurdwara* this became a loud jingle-jangle mixed up with their snorting. The odour of the latrines was replaced by the odour of mule-droppings.

The *gurdwara,* with its motley collections of pilgrims and other guests in its dozen rooms, was a small world of its own.

I was not on visiting terms with any of the other residents, but there were some one could not avoid. Next door to me were

126

two brothers, both Sikhs. The only way I could tell which was the older was by their beards. The older man's beard reached down to his navel; the younger one's covered his chest. Besides that, the elder brother's beard was almost grey: the younger one had only a few silver streaks in the mass of black. Both had their heads covered with loosely tied turbans and wore long, shapeless coats. They started their mornings by spreading out trays full of medicinal herbs and arguing about their merits at the tops of their voices. They spent the whole day hawking these herbs. Even if their herbs did not cure people, they did not kill them either. No one came to charge them with homicide. Every evening they would grind hashish and drink a cup or two of *bhang*. Occasionally they had guests — usually the caretakers of the *gurdwara*. And if the brothers had a good day in the bazaar, they brought sweets to offer their guests, along with the potion brewed from the green herb.

I had to pass the main kitchen on my way out of the *gurdwara*. I always exchanged a few words with the two Nihangs who had assumed charge of the *langar* feeding arrangements.

In the days when Ranjit Singh was Maharajah of Punjab, Akali Phula Singh had enlisted Nihangs and fought fierce battles with the Afghans and Pathans. The Nihang fraternity had descended from those warriors. But now there were no battles to fight. So they simply consumed *bhang*. The word Nihang means crocodile; the two men in the kitchen certainly resembled these monsters. The only work entrusted to the Nihangs was to cook lentils and vegetables and bake *chappaties* on the large, flat iron grill. This was the Guru's kitchen where everyone had to be fed free — whether for a day or for a month no one could prescribe. The Guru's kitchen was like a club where the only qualification for membership was a ravenous appetite.

The *gurdwara* also had a *granthi;* everyone addressed him as *Gyaniji.* Every visitor had to see him; without his permission no one could stay in the premises. Every evening when he went round to inspect the rooms we exchanged news. He wore a white turban and carried a saffron scarf about his neck with which he constantly wiped his nose; he always seemed to have a cold — or at least the illusion of one. He rubbed his nose so often that it had become raw and inflamed. His voice was feminine and melodious. He spoke so softy that people had to strain their ears to catch his words.

At 10 p.m. it started to rain.

My neighbours, the vendors of medicinal herbs, were celebrating. It seemed that they had done well with their stomach powder which they claimed could help digest even wood or stone. There was quite a crowd in their room. And they all spoke in Punjabi at the top of their voices, hurling full-blooded abuse at each other. The tone of bravado and the slurring over words left no doubt in my mind that they had imbibed liberal quantities of the green herb. All at once they stopped talking. I sat up with a jerk. A voice laden with pathos sang a couplet of Tegh Bahadur, the 9th of the Sikh's ten gurus:

Worry not about death; all who are born must die;
Worry only over events which are not likely to pass.

I had heard this *sloka* many a time in the *gurdwaras* but it had never affected me the way it did that night, sung in that melancholy voice.

Suddenly the lights went off. There was a roar of protests from different rooms. Some of the residents were prepared for the eventuality and had provided themselves with candles; others ran out to the *bazaar* to buy them. The singing next door did not betray any concern over the crisis.

I shut the book I was reading and flung it on my bed. I went out of my room and stood by the railing. I ignored the malodorous vapours coming up from the latrines. I looked inside the open door of the neighbouring room. They had a fat candle burning in the centre. Around the candlelight I could see a variety of beards like a circle of watches around a cauldron. It was then that I noticed that the singer was no other than Soorma Singh. Even in that hour of the night he wore his dark glasses. His long hair had slipped out from under his turban and was scattered about his pock-marked face. He lifted his face towards the ceiling as he sang. I could see the muscles of his neck flex as his voice rose or fell.

I stayed out on the balcony till Soorma Singh stopped singing.

The two Nihangs were very conscious of their importance. They spent their day in the kitchen. Whenever they met a new visitor they would tell him: 'We were on our way to Hemkund. We stopped here because this is also the abode of the *Guru*. *Gyaniji* won't let us leave.'

On the way to Badrinath beyond Rishikesh is the lake Hemkund. It was here that the 10th Guru, Gobind Singh, meditated before he decided to come into the world. Whenever the Nihangs were upset they packed up their belongings and threatened to leave for Hemkund. Then *Gyaniji* would come, blowing his nose into his scraf, and persuade them to stay. The Nihangs were easily persuaded. *Gyaniji* would then return to his room — blowing his nose into his scarf.

It did not take very much to upset the Nihangs. They had never worked in a kitchen. But there was nothing else they could do; so they were charged with the duty of cooking the meals. The first thing they did in the morning was to light the fires of the cooking range. Those for cooking the sacred *halva* had large cauldrons on them; another fire, equally large, was filled with black lentils and third one had a cannister of water for brewing tea. Someday the lentils were like clear soup. Somedays they had more grit than salt; on others it was just grit without any salt. And if they had nothing to do, the Nihangs would take their long iron prongs and pace about the kitchen, like warriors at sword-play.

In the afternoons and evenings, the kitchen became the centre of great bustle and activity. There was never a shortage of beggars who spent the time between meals picking lice out of their rags. There were two reasons for their assembling before the food was ready. One was to get round the Nihangs and the other, to get their share of the lentils: as the lentil cauldron emptied, the proportion of grit in what remained increased.

Soorma Singh's main duty was to sing hymns. In his spare time he took it upon himself to impart religious advice. After every two sentences he would exclaim, *'Wahe Guru, wahe Guru.'*

The Nihangs were crude rustics with little respect for anyone — least of all for Soorma Singh. Nevertheless Soorma Singh would go uninvited to the kitchen and take his seat on a board, a little removed from the fire. He was well aware of the fact that no one paid any heed to what he said; nevertheless he could not refrain from proffering gratuitous advice on the art of cooking. His major complaint was the excess of salt in the lentils. This used to irritate the Nihangs who had no doubt whatsoever in their minds that they were the best cooks in the world. Who was Soorma Singh to tell them what to do! If he grumbled about the food, they would snap back at him. *'Oi, you think your bloody woman is cooking for you!'*

Such remarks evoked many a smile. But the taunt about his wife produced a thunderous expression on Soorma Singh's face. He would grind his teeth and mutter, 'I hate talking to women.'

'Ho, ho,' one of the Nihangs would roar, giving his moustache a twist, 'You won't talk to women; and women won't have anything to do with you.'

Soorma Singh's ear would go red. Once the Nihangs started on this subject, there was no stopping them. 'This Soorma Singh is a dark horse. If you don't believe me you can see him at it any morning after service. When the women sit in the courtyard to take the sun, old Soorma Singh finds his way into their midst. He loves women's gossip; isn't that so, old Soorma? What do you get out of hearing old wives tales? ...and Mr. Soorma Singh keeps a hawk's eye on the other end of the courtyard; that's where the women wash their clothes. He keeps wandering about the place. He runs into one, trips over another. Great man you are, Mister Soorma Singh, a truly great man.'

The Nihangs would join the palms of their hands and make deep obeisance. Then the other would take over the narrative... 'Only the other day... isn't she the wife of that fellow Sajjan Singh?...the big buxom wench! Well, she was washing her clothes. Our dear friend Soorma Singh proceeded that way on the pretext of fetching water from the tap. And then let his foot slip so that he fell squarely on the lady. He was too hurt to be able to get up in a hurry. That one is a bit of a shrew. She wrenched off the turban of Sardar Bahadur Soorma Singh, caught him by his large top-knot, dragged him out of the bathroom and clipped him on his skull with her slipper, four or five real sharp ones. Meanwhile her husband arrived on the scene. He was in a rage. He would surely have sent Soorma Singh to the next world but for the people who intervened and restored peace. Poor, poor Soorma Singh! Take off your turban and let's see how many hairs remain on your scalp after the shoe-beating.'

The roar of laughter would frighten the mules tethered outside the *gurdwara*. Someone would break in gently. 'The poor fellow can't see a thing. Even if a woman were to stand in front of him without a stitch of clothing on her, what difference would it make to him?'

This was never said to help Soorma Singh but to encourage the Nihangs. One would say with great conviction. 'He doesn't have to see anything; he gets all his fun by the sound. He can tell a women's age, her looks, her secret desires — everything, by the way she speaks...'

There was a small balcony on the second floor. It was not plastered; lines of cement ran zig-zag across the bare brick floor. Along the wall were four bathrooms without doors; the bathers could be seen from the outside. Each bathroom had a tap. Water ran in them only for a couple of hours of the day; for the rest, if one turned on the tap, all one would get was a few spluttering sounds. In the middle of the balcony was a platform built round a wooden mast on which hung a very limp, a very beard-like, triangular saffron flag. If the breeze was strong, the flag would unfurl and display the emblems of the Khalsa — the circular *quou* with sabres crossed beneath it. At one end of the balcony was a curved steel railing; from this railing one got a view of the valley with the kites wheeling below. One could also see the road winding up the hillside through the damp vegetation, and long lines of mules with the muleteers holding on to the tails of their beasts to haul themselves up.

I caught sight of Soorma Singh in a shaft of sunlight, coming towards me. He was wearing a clean white turban and a freshly washed shirt. Instead of his native slipper he had a pair of shining pumps on his feet. He still wore his dark glasses — he probably slept in them.

I happened to be in the shop of Bhutia. His wares consisted of an assortment of things of Bhutanese make — kitchen utensils, cheap jewellery, idols, metal trays and other bric-a-brac. The Bhutia had taken me for a rich man and raised his prices so high that I had lost interest in his goods and was looking at the hillside. There were no houses on the other side of the road: only a twenty-feet-high wall made of rough blocks of stone that ran along the embankment. The wall was covered with moss and a large number of lady-birds crawled on the moss; it looked a green carpet with tiny red flowers.

That was when I saw Soorma Singh. I was surprised at the pace at which he walked; even people who could see, seldom walked as fast. Either he did not know how people walked or he wanted to give the impression that he could walk as well as those who could see. As he passed by me, I noticed that he had a cage dangling in one hand. Inside the cage was a green parrot peering out of the bars.

'That parrot,' the older Nihang told me later, scratching the hair on his chest, 'means the world to Soorma Singh; its all he has — it is his father, mother, sister, son, wife, elder-uncle, mother's brother, brothers...everything.'

The Nihang spoke with great contempt. He did not realise that Soorma Singh's lonely life had impressed me. He didn't even bother to look my way. He was watching the lentil cauldron which was boiling over, like lava pouring out of a volcano. Streaks of lentils flowed down the side of the cauldron and sizzled to a dry stop as they were scorched by the fire below.

There was no point my telling the Nihang what I thought of Soorma Singh. To be quite truthful. I had not really given much thought to Soorma Singh. Only when I ran into him, did I dwell on him for a few moments. I could tell from the expression on the Nihang's face that he was eager to talk to me. To encourage him I asked: 'Can the parrot talk?'

133

'Yes Sir! Soorma Singh has taught him a lot of things.'

'Soorma Singh recites couplets of Guru Tegh Bahadur. He must have crammed his parrot with verses of Bulhey Shah and Baba Farid,' I suggested.

'No sir... he has not taught his parrot any such thing.'

'Nihang Singhji, what has he taught his parrot to say?'

'It says: "Come Sardar Manjeet Singhji." That's his real name...no one bothers with his real name. He is just Soorma Singh to everyone. Some people even call him *Soormua* Singh.' The Nihang smiled and explained his joke. '*Soormua* means one with a pig's snout.' He continued. 'He's taught the bird many other things. Sentimental sentences and words of love.'

The younger Nihang took up the narrative. 'My friend has also taught the parrot many kinds of abuse — "Soorma is a woman chaser; Soorma Singh is a great rascal; Soorma Singh is a real bastard..." '

I wanted to change the subject. There was no way of doing so except by breaking out in loud laughter.

The elder Nihang noticed my discomfiture. He made a wry face and said. 'Sir, this Soorma Singh is a big nuisance. He does not like lentils. If I cook a vegetable, he turns up his nose; and he finds faults with our chappaties. It never crosses his mind that we are not cooks. He should take the name of the great Guru and eat whatever is placed before him.'

I agreed that Soorma Singh should eat whatever came from the Guru's kitchen without making a fuss. 'If Soorma Singh does not like the *gurdwara* food, why doesn't he cook his own?' I asked.

'That's exactly what we feel too. But *Gyaniji* indulges him too much. He sings a couple of hymns in the morning service and *Gyaniji* thinks he is the greatest singer in the world. He has given Soorma Singh a separate room to live in.'

The other Nihang butted in, 'You can hardly call it a room! Next to the latrines is a tiny store-room to stack wood, coal, flour, lentils and other kitchen rations. In one corner of this room Sardar Soorma Singh has laid his charpoy and hung his parrot cage.'

One night at about 10 p.m. the parrot began to squawk. I had never heard the bird before, but that night it was screaming as if a tiger had entered the cage. Many people came out of their rooms to find out what had happened. Then Soorma Singh also began to yell at the parrot. We could not hear what they were saying to each other.

The uproar continued for some time. Then Soorma Singh's voice could be heard crying — 'Help! Murder! He's killing me.'

I took my flashlight and ran down the stairs. I saw the older Nihang run out of Soorma Singh's room and disappear in the darkness of the latrines.

Soorma Singh continued to scream for help. Other people came on the scene. We took Soorma Singh to the first floor. He was suffering from shock. It appeared that one of the Nihangs had stolen into his room in the dark and tried to strangle him with his scarf.

Gyaniji was aroused by the din and came on the scene. The older Nihang who had quietly slipped back into his room was summoned. He explained that all he had done was to take food to Soorma Singh's room and then returned to his own. He did not know what transpired after he had left.

It was obvious that the Nihang was lying. Even so someone came to his defence. 'Soorma Singh is always bothering these poor chaps. They spend all their day serving in the Guru's kitchen and then His Lordship expects to be served in his room.'

135

Soorma Singh leapt to his defence with all the power in his lungs. 'All these fellows gang up in the kitchen to make fun of me; the Nihangs are particularly nasty to me. Sometimes they urinate in my lentil soup; at other times they'll deliberately char my chappaties and slap them on my face. Just now when one of them brought me dinner he said "Here, you bastard, you parasite"...'

There was a commotion. Soorma Singh abused the Nihangs with all his might. *Gyaniji* pleaded with him, 'If you go on yelling like this, you will lose your voice. How will you be able to sing tomorrow morning?'

The exchange of hot abuse was followed by soft words of peace. The Nihangs again threatened to leave for HemKund. *Gyaniji* dissuaded them from doing so. He wiped his nose with his scarf. My neighbours, the vendors of medicinal herbs, took Soorma Singh to their room while *Gyaniji* cooled the tempers of the Nihangs and sent them back to their quarters.

A few days later there was another party in the room next door. Amongst the distinguished company I espied the two Nihangs and Soorma Singh. Green jade cups were being passed round. I could also hear endearing abuse such as is used by friends for each other. This was Soorma Singh in a new incarnation, so different from the Soorma Singh of everyday life. His turban had fallen off his head and lay entangled between his legs; his beard was scattered untidily; his top-knot had loosened and his long hair lay about his shoulders; his dark glasses lay in his lap. He was flailing his arms like a windmill and bellowing like a mad bull. One would have thought that the houris of paradise were performing a nautch right in front of his sightless eyes. The party were pleading with him for couplets from Bulhey Shah or Baba Farid.

Soorma Singh made a few attempts to sing, but he was too drunk to get the notes right and the attempts ended in a camel-like hurrumph. The failure angered Soorma Singh. He leapt to his feet, slapped his chest: '*Hai*, I am smitten!'

A chorus of voices demanded : 'True Emperor! who could dare to smite you?'

Soorma Singh was in a world of his own. All he could say in reply was to repeat '*Hai*, I am smitten!'

The Nihangs sprinkled some cold water on Soorma Singh's head — 'You are hot in the head Soorma Singh! Repeat the name of the great God, *Wahe Guru.*'

The drops of cold water acted like magic. He put his hand over his ear and in his tear-laden voice sang:

'Farid wake from the slumber! thy beard hath turned grey.
The future lies ahead of thee, the past is passed away.'

The men began to sway in ecstasy; their beards also swayed with them. Their eyes closed and a drunken stupor overcame them. Once Soorma Singh had begun, there was no stopping him; wherever his voice carried, it cast its spell. He had a vast repertoire of *slokas* beginning with 'Farid, wake from thy slumber!' He sang into the late hours of the night.

It was the magic of Soorma Singh's voice which compelled an agnostic like me to go to the prayer hall every morning.

The *gurdwara* prayer hall was very spacious. Its bare white walls dazzled the eye. The floor was covered with coir matting on which was spread a blue *durrie* with a red border. On one side of the hall on a raised platform was the holy *Granth*. Usually *Gyaniji* sat on the platform. Behind him would be a boy waving the fly whisk. Above the *Granth* was a coloured awning festooned with red and yellow tassels. A couple of dozen large pictures were hung on the walls; some of these were of the Sikh *Gurus;* other depicted scenes from Sikh history.

When Soorma Singh entered the crowded hall, the congregation would be tense with excitement. On these occasions Soorma Singh dressed with great care; a clean white shirt and *chooridars* of handspun *khaddar*, a round white turban on his head, a blue scarf round his neck — and the dark glasses with their lenses and frame glistening brightly. He also wore socks on these occasions. Instead of his staff, he would have his tambourin which he used as an accompaniment. People said that Soorma Singh's renderings of the sacred hymns had pierced many a deaf ear and guided the listeners along the true and narrow path of religion.

This was not very incredible. If confirmed agnostics like me could be moved, those who were only wavering in their faith must surely have had their doubts cleared... I must admit that although his singing used to disturb me, it instilled peace in the minds of most people. I could seldom catch the words of the hymns. His voice had the force and flow of a hill torrent, the deep gloom of unseen, unknown caverns of the ocean ...I cannot really describe the quality of his voice except that to me Soorma Singh was nothing except his voice. It reflected his loneliness, his utter solitude in the wide, wide world, his agitated search, his unquenched thirst, his unappeased hunger; it was the cry of his soul, an agonising cry which rang through the melody of his songs...

The sun had set behind a haze of clouds; only a dim glow lit the mountains.

The foreman gave my belongings a quick appraising look and asked, 'How many coolies will you require?'

'One.'

'Are you alone?'

'Yes, I am alone.'

He began calculating the load the coolie would have to carry. I was on my bed reading a book; my small attache case was hidden underneath. I shut the book and explained, 'There is only one bedding roll and a small suitcase.' I got up and lifted the edge of the bed sheet. The foreman bent down to gauge the size of the case. 'That will be two rupees, Sahib.'

'How long will it take to get to the bus stand?'

'Fifteen minutes less than an hour.'

'Don't forget I have to get on the 8.00 a.m. bus. The coolie should be here by a quarter to seven.'

'*Accha* Sahib.'

The words '*accha* Sahib' kept going round my head long after the foreman had gone. When I found the page of my book, I had to close the book. Once again there was an uproar. There was always an uproar of some kind or the other. It could be hymn-singing, quarrels between the women, the screaming of children. But this was from the ground floor, from Soorma Singh's room. Were the Nihangs up to their tricks again?

My one thought was to save the voice of Soorma Singh. I leapt out of bed and went to the door. I saw the two Nihangs in the kitchen sipping tea out of their porcelain mugs. 'What is the racket?' I asked them.

They paused and listened. I ran down the steps. The noise was coming from Soorma Singh's room. A small crowd had collected there. I looked in. A fat, ugly woman of about thirty-four was squatting on a charpoy with Soorma Singh on his knees on the floor beside her. A Sikh with a goatee was slapping Soorma Singh about the face.

This fellow was an urban type — short, pot-bellied, flabby, with small thin arms and hands like squirrel's claws.

'What's going on?' demanded a chorus of voices.

The Sikh with the goatee panted, 'This man was staring at my wife...even after I told him to look the other way.'

In short, Soorma Singh's crime was to have stared at the loathsome creature with eyes like hard-boiled eggs and a skin the colour of mud.

Gyaniji threaded his way through the crowd and came up to the man with the goatee. He put out his inflamed proboscis and protested. 'Sir, this is Soorma Singh, he has no eyes. How could he have been gaping at anyone? There was no other room vacant, that is why I put you in his room. Where else can the poor fellow go?...'

Soorma Singh's glasses had fallen off but his assailant had not bothered to look at his eyes. His wife was very cross and scolded her husband — 'You never wait to find out anything before you get down to fisticuffs.'

The Sardarji was like a deflated balloon; he looked exactly like a squirrel with a beard. It was obvious that he was dominated by his wife. Some explanations were offered; the Sardarji picked up his bag and slipped out to go to the *bazaar* to buy vegetables, *Gyaniji* went to the door and spoke to the onlookers, 'Gentlemen go and do your own work... this is not juggler's performance.'

Gyaniji's thin nasal voice commanded respect. The crowd dispersed. *Gyaniji* turned and admonished the woman with the bulging eyes, 'Sister, Soorma Singh has a golden voice. You have arrived today; come to the service tomorrow morning and listen to him singing hymns. There is such magic in his voice that many who have gone astray, have been brought back to the path of righteousness.'

Just then the parrot made a few uncomplimentary remarks about Soorma Singh. *Gyaniji* glowered at the bird. His nose was as red as the parrot's beak.

Gyaniji explained to the woman that this was the Nihang's handiwork. Soorma Singh's cup of sorrow brimmed over. He voiced a whole catalogue of the misdeeds of the Nihangs. The woman asked, 'Soorma Singhji, whose word shall I accept, the *Gyaniji's* or the parrot's?'

'That's a very odd question to ask,' protested *Gyaniji* and left the room still mauling his nose.

A small multi-coloured bird landed on the window sill and danced a pirouette.

There was tenderness, humility and sweetness in the woman's voice; it pierced through the deep dark of Soorma Singh's world like a shaft, making a silver track as it went — a path which appeared to Soorma Singh to be leading to his goal.

the nuptial bed

Upendra Nath Ashk

Keshi looked up from his newly-wedded wife's eyes to the head-board of the old-fashioned bed, in which was framed a miniature of his mother. She was a lovely woman, fine-featured with large eyes and curling lashes; a smile hovered on her slightly parted lips, revealing a row of pearl-white teeth. Unconsciously his mother's image was projected on that of his bride's. How closely the two women resembled each other! His head went into a whirl; a shiver ran down his body. He shook his head vigorously and tried to take his eyes off the picture. It was of no avail.

Till a few years ago, he had lain on his mother's bosom just as he was now lying on his wife's. The memories of those years came flooding back into his mind. Instead of kissing his bride's almond eyes and eager lips, he slid off her body and lay down beside her like one utterly exhausted. He stared at the long strings of jasmine beads which hung like a canopy over his bed. His hand fell on the jasmine petals which were spread like a thick counterpane over the bed sheets. He wanted to leap from his bed and break out of the fragrant nuptial room in which he found himself imprisoned.

Keshi did not jump off the bed. He lay where he was, still and silent. What would his bride think! That fear alone kept him on the nuptial bed. He shook his head again, even more violently than before. But instead of ridding his mind of his mother's image, it produced a myriad more, which came tumbling down through the spate.

...It is the same bed in the same room. His parents are lying side by side. He is staring at them from his cot in the verandah. How petite and pretty his mother looks beside his father.

...His mother is doing her hair in front of the mirror. He stares at her from behind the door. She is as beautiful as the fairy that his *ayah* tells of in her stories. His mother, seeing his reflection in the mirror, asks him to come to her. He goes to her and buries his face in her lap. She ruffles his hair with one hand and continues to comb her own with the other.

...What's wrong with Papa? A man comes in to see him everyday. He has a pair of snakes hanging round his neck. He puts the tails of the serpents in his ears and feels Papa's chest with their head. Then he sticks long needles in Papa's arms. Papa does not cry but Keshi begins to howl. His mother clasps him to bosom and takes him to the next room.

...Papa is lying on the floor. He does not move. Everyone is crying. His mother is crying; she kisses him and continues to cry. Women help his mother to break all her bangles and then wipe off the vermillion in the parting of her hair. They drag Keshi out of her lap. He shrieks and howls but no one bothers to comfort him.

...It is the same bed. He lies where his Papa had lain before him. His mother is beside him. She is dressed in a plain, white sari. The morning sun is streaming through the fanlight but she sleeps on, without a care in the world. He stares at her face. Her features are truly as delicate as a fairy's. Her eyes are closed, her hair scattered about her shoulders. She is like the princess who was woken out of her spell by Prince Charming. He edges towards her and kisses her on the cheek. She opens her eyes, stretches her arms and takes him in her embrace. She kisses him on his forehead, eyes and lips.

...He lies with his head on his mother's bosom. She tells him the story of the prince who crossed the seven seas to marry the princess of his heart's desire. She finishes the story and asks him. 'Will you marry a princess?'

'I will marry you.'

'Silly boy! Whoever heard of a son marrying his mother!'

She promises him that she will find him a bride just like herself.

'Then I will have this bed as well,' he says looking at his mother's beautiful portrait in the head-rest.

'Yes, of course! This bed will be my wedding present to you and your bride.'

'What's the matter? Aren't you feeling well?' His bride turns over, feels his forehead and runs her fingers through his hair.

'It's nothing at all,' he answers shaking his head to snap the chain of thought. He tries to laugh, it turns into a long sigh.

His mother had been true to her word. The bride that she had chosen for him was an exact image of herself — slender and comely. Her eyes were large, her features clear cut, het lips soft and her teeth glistened like a row of pearls. A large bed had been sent with the dowry; but his mother had fulfilled her old vow and laid out her own precious bed for him to consummate his wedlock. She had even given up her own bedroom to the bridal pair.

The bride bent over her groom. She gazed into his eyes to see if she could find out why his ardour had cooled so suddenly;

but she got no closer to the truth. She hesitated a little; then began to fondle his hair.

For a while Keshi lay still; then he put his arms round his bride's neck and drew her close to him. He stroked her hair, her cheeks and her lips. The cobwebs were swept out of his mind. The soft, fair body of the woman imparted some of its warmth to him and hot blood began to course in his veins. He kissed her, laid her beside him and buried his face in her warm breasts. It was time he made love to his newly wedded wife, he thought, but he could not bring himself to face the picture. Without raising his head he pushed his pillow against the head-board. Then he looked up. His mother's face still peered at him from behind the pillow. 'No, no, no,' he cried within himself and again lay on his back like one defeated. Angry with himself he leapt out of the nuptial bed.

The full moon sieved through the *chick*-curtain; and lit the verandah with a soft silvery light. Keshi paused by the niche and looked at the moon-beams playing on the lawn. The cool breeze soothed his overwrought nerves. He went out into the garden amongst the beds of phlox and verbena. Dahlias, heavy with their own weight swayed in the breeze. Bordering the lawn was a neatly pruned hedge of *henna*, and beyond it a bed of marigolds. A rambler rose climbed in spirals over a cluster of nasturtiums. Keshi examined some of the flowers, smelt some and caressed the others. In the daylight these flowers dazzled the eyes with their gaudy colours; now they were soft in the moonlight, like a balm for strained nerves. The bright yellows and pinks had turned pale whites; the deep crimsons, the blues and the mauves were repainted in sombre hues.

Keshi came to the cottage wall where the jasmine blossomed. In the dark shadow of the wall, the jasmine flowers gleamed like petalled pearls. Jasmines in moonlight reminded him of the lines of a song:

'After a long time the jasmine has blossomed
My courtyard is filled with fragrance,
A heavenly fragrance.'

Now that his courtyard was in fact fragrant, the words of
the song were lost in a pit of oblivion. Keshi walked stiffly up
and down between the cottage and the gate. When he was
walking back to the cottage for the second time he noticed a
light in the window of the corner room. His mother had
obviously not gone to bed. Perhaps his aunt and other
kinswomen were also awake discussing him and his bride. What
infinite pains his mother had taken in decorating his nuptial
bed! The women had cleared the dining room of the table and
chairs and adorned it to receive the bride. They had carried out
the ceremonial connected with the reception of a new bride,
lifting her veil with infinite care. While he sat amongst his
friends, they were arranging the wedding presents, and the
furniture, which had been received in the dowry, in his room
and also decorating his mother's room for the first night of the
married couple. The innumerable guests and the hundred odds
and ends to attend to, had given his mother little time for sleep.
He had seen her going in and out of her bedroom with his aunt
and a young woman who was a distant cousin of his mother's,
busy in their task of beautifying the bridal suite. His mother's
face was lit with joyful radiance. It seemed that the sleepless
nights, the running about and the endless bother about
everything were in fact all centred round the embellishment of
that one room. Many a time he went in on some pretext or the
other to see what his mother and aunt were up to, but each time
they bustled him out: even a casual glance at the room was
forbidden till the nuptial night.

Often while talking to his friends during the wedding
ceremonies, or listening to women's banter, Keshi's eyes would
settle on his mother. Although she was nearing forty and the

twenty-two years of widowhood had hardened her expression and etched dark rings around her eyes, the wedding of her only child seemed to have wrought a miracle in her. Not a trace of fatigue showed on her face; the circles around her eyes had vanished. She looked exquisite in her white sari. To Keshi she was the most beautiful of all women he had ever seen.

Keshi feared that the fatigue and the sleepless nights would make his mother ill. Every night before he retired he would go to her and plead, 'Mother, go to bed now!' Far from resting herself she would instead come to his bed, gently rub oil on his temples and brow till he fell asleep. Then she would go back to her work.

Keshi had formed a habit of having oil rubbed into his scalp. During his examinations when he stayed up all night and wanted a couple of hours of sleep during the day, his mother would rub oil on his head. Even then Keshi, unable to stop gazing at her, would refuse to fall asleep. His mother would press the palms of her hands on his eyes and kiss them; she would run her fingers across his forehead, their soft silken touch laden with love that gradually made his lids heavy with sleep and at last he would fall into a deep slumber.

Keshi had learnt this art from her. Whenever his mother had insomnia because she was tired or worried, he would sit by her pillow and rub oil behind her ears till she fell asleep. When he was younger — thirteen or fourteen — his mother would often pull his head down and kiss him on his lips. When he grew into manhood, got his bachelor's and then his master's degree and was appointed professor of psychology in the local college, his mother began kissing his forehead instead of his lips.

All through the festivities Keshi wished he could rescue his mother from the crowd of women who had come to the wedding, lift her up bodily and force her to go to bed. But there she was as busy as ever, weaving garlands around the nuptial bed. When the flowers ran out she sent out people all over the town to bring more. She squandered money as it were of no value. He wanted to say to her, '*Ma*, why take all this trouble at the expense of your health? Your love means more to me than these ceremonial festivities, more than all these festoons and garlands. You mean more to me than such things. You will make yourself ill.' But he knew that she would pay no heed to what he said. 'Son, my own wedding was a non-descript sort of affair,' she had told him when he tried to protest. 'Your father was only a low-paid clerk; he hadn't yet taken the competitive examination for the covenanted service. I do not want your bride to have any regrets. You just wait and see how lavishly I shall decorate the nuptial-bed for your bride!'

His aunt had pushed him on to the bed and said with a laugh, 'Don't you waste your time expounding philosophy!' It took him some time to catch the insinuation.

He had had this room for a long time and he was familiar with everything in it — the bed and the rest of the furniture. His mother's dressing table, her vanity case, her papier mache bangle box, her table lamp for which she had paid a tidy sum in Bombay, had been left just as they always had been. What made it look brighter were the garlands of jasmine buds — the first of the season. They were hung in long strings round a canopy frame to look like a floral mosquito net. They were also spread thick over the bed sheets. His bride lay on them like the goddess Flora. Her face was half-covered by her veil. The bed sheet was a virginal white.

Keshi imagined the scene of his mother's wedding. She was the bride of a low grade clerk in the canal department. It must have been in a hovel, on a coarse stringed charpoy; in the dim light of a hurricane lantern. It all seemed so hazy and dream-like. Later, his father had risen to the post of an executive engineer, and then his mother had had everything she wanted. But she never forgot the disappointment of her wedding night. She had adorned her son's nuptial-bed as she would have liked her own to have been. In this way she was fulfilling a desire which had been frustrated. But in so doing she had unwittingly wrought instruments of torture for her son. Whichever way he turned in that bedroom, memories of past days came crowding into his mind.

'Be sure not to waste your time expounding philosophy.' His aunt's words and her laughter echoed in his brain...Was he caught up in a web of his own fancy? What was his bride thinking? He thought of the many lives which he had heard were tragically destroyed by the groom's impotence on the first night. But was it necessary for a man to prove his manhood on the first night of his marriage? Why did women set such store by it? Did they take a vicarious pleasure in preparing the bed, and live their own nuptial night over again? Did his mother also...?

The trouble she was taking in decorating the bed giving up her own for the purpose... bedecking it with flowers to demonstrate what her own nuptial-bed should have looked like — if her husband's poverty and other obligations had not robbed her of the pleasure... Keshi beat his head violently with his fist. What was wrong with him? Why had he asked his mother for that bed? Yet he was only a child when he had asked. His mother should have known better.

He went back into the verandah. He saw his bride standing by the alcove. 'Are you not feeling well?' she asked him anxiously.

'I am all right.'

'Have I upset you in any way?'

Keshi wanted to laugh out as loudly as he could; even his wife had just one obsession. He put his arm round her waist and led her indoors, resolving firmly to lay aside his complexes and do what was expected of him. He pushed her on to the bed leaned over her and snapped open the buttons of her blouse.

She had put the pillow back in its place. And once more Keshi's eyes fell on his mother's picture. And once more his brain became fuddled. He shook himself free and rose from the bed. His wife caught at his hand.

'What is the matter?'

Keshi glanced towards the door. How much easier it would have been if his mother had decorated his room instead of her own! His room was stacked with furniture received in the dowry, and other oddments collected for the wedding. He did not even have the key of his room. Keshi cast a dispirited glance towards the verandah. Moonbeams played on the floor. He exclaimed: 'Look, how lovely it is in the moonlight! Let's take a stroll outside.'

The bride rose and re-adjusted her clothes. She took a quick glance in the mirror, tidied her hair, drew her veil across her forehead and followed her husband.

They strolled up to the gate and back to the verandah twice without speaking to each other. She tried to break the ice by saying something about the moonlight, but Keshi made no response; the two continued to stroll in silence.

The heady spring moonlight did not change their mood. The bride was perplexed at her groom's extraordinary behaviour. From her girl friends (some of whom were now mothers) she had heard of what happened between newly married couples on the first night. Her husband had started in the same way and then suddenly changed his mind. She had heard people praise his good looks, his learning, his gentleness. He was a lecturer at the university. Her father had made enquiries about him not only from his fellow lecturers, but also from the students and had only finalised the marriage negotiations after he was fully satisfied. No one had suggested that the boy was eccentric or slightly unhinged. Yet when she thought of him in his efforts to make love, her future seemed extremely bleak to her. Glancing furtively at him, she continued to walk beside him, barely noticing the lovely moonlight.

And Keshi's mind was like a quagmire; he could not find a way out of his dilemma. He continued his monotonous pacing with his hands clasped behind him as if they were chained to each other. When they came to the gate again he spoke brusquely, 'Come, let's go out for a while.'

'It is rather late,' she protested gently.

Keshi recalled that one of his friends, relating an amorous affair, had told him that the lane between the water tank and the Grand Trunk Road was lonely and shaded — an ideal place for lovers...

'Only as far as the water tank,' he pleaded.

He opened the gate. His bride followed him in trustful silence. Keshi began to explain the topography: It was once an exclusive residential area for senior English officials of the Railway; after Independence the bungalows had been taken over by Indians. When they passed by the flour mill, he explained to her how wheat and corn were ground. At the cold storage plant he recounted how 40,000 *maunds* of potatoes could be kept, to be marketed out of season. When they came to the press building, he peered through the window-panes and loudly began to explain the miracle of the rotary machine: how a blank sheet went in at one end and emerged at the other as a newspaper. He was heading for the railway station when he recalled what his friend had said about the lane connecting the water tank and the Grand Trunk Road. They turned towards the gate of the level crossing. It was closed. Keshi saw the red light and explained: 'This gate is an awful nuisance. There is always some train or the other passing through. The station had been extended, but no one has bothered with this gate. They should have an over-bridge here.'

There was still some time for the train. They crossed the line by a side gate and came to the water-tank. The right half of the road was open and lighted; the other half was dark. When Keshi turned towards the dark, his wife protested, 'Let's go home; it is very late,' but Keshi put his right arm round her waist. 'Just a little further,' he coaxed, 'see how the moon comes through the branches!'

'Why not the other side? It is a wide open road.'

'Are you scared?' he mocked gently, bending over to kiss her forehead.

The girl shook herself free in embarrassment. 'What are you doing... right on the road...'

Keshi laughed. Once more he put his arm round her waist and exclaimed, 'Who on earth will see us here at this time of the night!' Again, he bent to kiss her, but before he could do so the head-lights of a motor caught them in a blinding glare; a truck roared past. Barely had they recovered when another truck came along — followed by a whole convoy of trucks. 'Lonely, quiet road indeed,' muttered Keshi himself. The romantic mood vanished.

'Let's go back,' pleaded the girl in a tearful voice. 'I am tired.'

'This is the main road; trucks and cars run at all hours of the day and night,' explained Keshi. 'Let's go to the M.T. Lines. The road up to the church should be quite deserted.'

'I am very tired,' she begged.

He took her firmly by the waist and led her towards the open road to the military training lines.

The bungalows on either side of the road were bathed in the moonlight; still, as if taken by surprise. Beneath, the trees, the light and the shade were like fretwork forming a new pattern each time a gust of breeze shook the branches. Keshi tried to guess where the Queen-of-the-night blossomed; it breathed its fragrance into the atmosphere. He twined his arm round his wife's waist and took her under the shade of the trees.

'Are you very tired?' he asked.

She did not answer, but put her head against her husband's chest. He drew her face to his and kissed her on the lips.

The beam of a torch flashed from across the road; the couple sprang apart. Keshi went pale; his heart began to beat rapidly. He remembered that no one was allowed to come to the M.T. Lines after midnight.

A group of soldiers in dark-green uniforms came by singing a song from the latest film they had seen.

'Are you the moon when it is full
Or the sun in its glory?
Whatever you be
By the grace of God you are matchless in beauty.'

Despite the moonlight they flashed the light of their torch on the couple.

Keshi had wanted to take his bride in his arms, look into her eyes and repeat the opening lines of the song: 'Are you the moon when it is full or the sun in its glory?' But the bad manners of the soldiers quelled the romantic upsurge. He remembered an incident in which a friend and his sister who came to dine at a bungalow in the M.T. Lines were involved. They hadn't realised how late it was and were unable to find a rickshaw. When they were walking homewards at half past twelve they were stopped by the soldiers. They had to go back to their hosts to prove they were brother and sister...

153

Before his bride said anything again about going back, Keshi turned his steps homewards. When the soldiers had flashed their torch on his bride's face, Keshi had been roused to such a temper that he wanted to grip the fellow by the collar and slap him on the face. But, had there been a scene and if anyone had asked what the professor and his bride were doing at the late hour in the deserted lane, what could he have replied? ...He had resisted the impulse and all his spleen was vented on his mother — on the bed she had given him — and on his impotence.

He walked back at a brisk pace; his bride followed, dragging her feet a few steps behind him. When he entered the gate, he slowed down. The girl, clearly annoyed, went ahead at a quickened step, leaving him to follow. When Keshi came into the bedroom she was lying on the bed. One end of her sari was on the floor. The low cut blouse revealed the contours of her soft, warm breasts. Keshi wanted to go down on his knees and put his head in her lap. But once again (and without any volition on his part) his eyes travelled from his bride to his mother's portrait.

He stood in the centre of the room lost in thought. The girl stared at the ceiling, tears brimming her eyes. Keshi glanced at the door to his room. 'Isn't this door bolted from the outside?'

'Yes,' she replied with her gaze still fixed on the ceiling. Keshi walked round the room twice. 'Where is the key?'

'Probably with aunty; she had all the furniture put inside.'

Keshi went out to the other end of the house. The light in his mother's bedroom had been switched off. The other women had obviously gone to sleep too. Should he wake up his mother? If the aunt happened to wake up too, she would make fun of him. He came back and walked about the bedroom for a while. He stole a glance at his bride. She was still gazing stonily at the ceiling. He went to the door of his bedroom and put his shoulder against it. The bottom latch was firm and would not yield. His mother always used bottom latch. If it had been the upper latch he could have smashed the glass pane on the top of the door and undone the bolt.

He stepped back and examined the door. Both sides had three panes of glass each and the woodwork. If he broke the third pane he could get his hand to the bottom latch. He wanted to smash the glass with his fist; but the thought of waking up his mother was like a cold shower. He clenched his fists and resumed his wanderings in the room. He went round a few times and again stopped in front of the door. He looked at its base. The right side was somewhat damaged. He peered more closely. A crack showed clearly through the paint. He squatted on the floor, rested his back against the bed and pressed his heel against the crack with all his strength. The bed slid backwards but the door did not yield.

The bride lay stiff and unmoving; her gaze remained fixed on the ceiling. She seemed to take no notice of the bed sliding. Keshi stole a glance at her. She turned towards him. Their eyes met. Wasn't there just a trace of contempt in her eyes? Didn't she look at him as if he were a little mad? An insane impulse possessed Keshi, his rational faculties vanishing into thin air. He leapt up and with one powerful blow smashed the central pane of the door. The glass splintered and fell on the other side.

The bride sat up with a start. A look of astonishment came on her face as she rose and stood by her husband. 'What on earth are you doing?' she asked irritably.

Keshi did not reply. He did not even look at her. He put his arms through the broken pane and undid the latch on the other side. The door yielded as he hit the pane. Holding it with his left hand, he carefully withdrew his right arm. Even so his elbow was scratched.

Blood began to ooze through his torn sleeve.

'*Hai,* what you have done!' The girl cried. At once her voice was full of concern. She looked around to see if she could find something to bandage the cut.

Keshi paid no heed to her. He pushed the door open with both his hands and went in, switching on the light. The room was packed with wedding presents and the dowry furniture — dressing table, almirah, bundles of clothes, trays of sweets and dried fruit. The bed that had been sent in the dowry was also there. It was loaded with all kinds of garments. He picked them up in both his arms and flung them on the couch.

The bride had come in behind him. In her eyes was not bewilderment but fear. Keshi turned round and put his hands on her shoulders. He gazed into her frightened eyes; then drew her to him and kissed her on the mouth. Through her fear, she felt her husband's indifference change suddenly to passion; she felt his hot breath behind her ears. Slowly her petrified limbs relaxed in his warm embrace and she began to fondle his hair.

Early next morning Keshi's mother woke up and came to the bridal chamber. Alarmed to see the door open, she tip-toed in and parted the curtain. What she saw, made her gasp. The decorated room was as empty as a mausoleum. Her eye fell on the other door and the splinters of glass on the floor and her alarm grew. Was there a robber in the house? She crept forward to see for herself. On the threshold she stopped dead in surprise. The bridal pair lay fast asleep on the rough unmade bed, with just the cushions of the sofa beneath them.

❄

happy new year
Ajeet Caur

A fter years of hammering away on typewriters, Kapoor's fate came to be linked with that of the Hon'ble Minister of the Central Government. Overnight his status was elevated from plain and simple Kapoor to Kapoor Sahib: Personal Assistant to the H.M. (Honourable Minister). In those few hours his chest expanded visibly by a couple of inches. When he strutted down the office corridors his breast puffed out like that of a crested bantam cock, it seemed as if corridors were not broad enough for him. Peons who usually sat on their stools chewing betel leaf or nodding with sleep would spring to attention and salute him as he passed.

The metamorphosis took place a few days before the year was to end. In the long years that Kapoor had been a clerk he had never as much as thought of such trifles as New Year's Eve or New Year's day. It had never occurred to him that the year which had been young a little while ago had aged and would soon give up the ghost. The thirty-firsts of December were no different from the thirtieths or thirty-firsts of other months: days of penniless penury. The firsts of January were like the firsts of all other months when he received his month's salary, paid off his debtors, fulfilled his childrens' oft-postponed demands for new exercise books, new textbooks, new pairs of socks to replace the old riddled with holes, school uniforms, pencils, etc. It was a strange mixture of sensations: an imperious feeling of governing other peoples' destinies as well as a diminution of stature which came with the realisation that before half the day was over more than half his salary would be eaten up.

After Kapoor had been transformed into Kapoor Sahib, his life style changed. How the transformation came about was very simple.

A businessman to be more exact, an industrialist who had done business with his Minister, arrived at the Ministerial residence armed with a New Year's gift. The date, 31st of December, Time: 8 a.m. Mr Kapoor was ensconced in a room in the outer verandah and seated in the chair of the Personal Assistant to the Hon'able Minister.

The Minister took one look at the parcel and remarked: 'Sorry, I have given up drink. You must know what the Prime Minister's views on the subject are. PM has ordered...'

The industrialist muttered an oath. Of course, only inside himself, but one which had reference to the Minister's relations with his own mother. He also felt apprehensive that the bugger might be trying to slip out of his grasp. However, he bared his entire denture in a broad smile and replied: 'Not at all, sir. I'll bring something else tomorrow or the day after. But this is New Year's Eve and I mustn't leave without an offering for you.' He opened his briefcase, took out a diary and placed it on the table before the Minister. It was a miserable little specimen printed in the government press. However, in its pages was a wad of other papers also bearing the imprint of the Government of India. The Minister opened the diary, felt the thickness of the wad of notes and remarked: 'You needn't have taken this trouble: it wasn't really necessary for you to put yourself out in this way.'

'No trouble at all, sir,' sniggered the industrialist. 'This is only to buy sweets for the children.'

It can be established that as a person rises in the world, his children's appetite for sweets and candies increases. The 'candy box' in the diary was worth more than a confectioner's shop crammed with goodies.

The Minister gave a wan smile baring two-and-a-half of his dentures and quietly slipped the diary in the drawer of his table.

The industrialist sighed with relief. It had been a touch-and-go affair. As he stepped out of the Minister's office he handed the parcel he had brought for the Minister to Kapoor. The Personal Assistant to the Minster had also to be kept happy. All this happened so quickly that Kapoor was neither able to protest nor as much as utter a word of thanks. It was the first time in his life that someone had considered him worthy of a gift of any kind.

He was somewhat ill at ease but the industrialist's voice as he left with a triumphant smile was most reassuring: 'It's a small gift for the New Year.' Kapoor's hands shook as he put the bottle in a drawer of his table. He felt hot all over his body.

Vashisht, the typist, shared the room with Kapoor. He had been the Minister's typist and had sat in the same corner for many years. On the very first day that Kapoor came to occupy his new chair, Vashisht had introduced himself with a reassuring smile: 'Do not worry sir, I will show you all the ropes. Ministers come to go; their job are not permanent. But your humble servant had been confirmed in his post and is quite familiar with the goings-on that take place in this room. I will not let any trouble come near you.'

Vashisht sensed Kapoor's discomfiture and casually walked up to him as he took a leaf of betel out of a wrap of paper. 'Congratulation Kapoor Sahib. The first gift is like the ceremony of removing the nose-ring of a bride. You must entertain your humble servants and thus ensure the grace of God. We will always pray for your health.'

Kapoor was novice at the game. He realised he could not drink an entire bottle of Scotch all by himself and was relieved to have someone share it with him: 'Sure! Sure!' he replied.

'Fine! This evening we'll welcome the New Year in your home as all the *burra* Sahibs do in big hotels. Singing and embracing each others' wives at the midnight hour. Can I also invite Gupta on your behalf?' Gupta was the second typist. He sat in another room which he shared with the two other clerks. Gupta was in charge of receiving and sorting out the mail; the other was responsible for the despatch.

'Sure!' replied Kapoor expansively.

Kapoor came home a little earlier than usual carrying the bottle of Scotch in his attache case. He was not prepared for the tongue-lashing his wife gave him. 'Did you have to bring this destroyer of families in our own home? And drink the evil stuff in the presence of children! New Year? What the hell is this New Year? Today is the thirty-first and there is neither a vegetable nor a scrap of a biscuit nor anything else to eat in the house. I am ashamed of asking the grocer for another loan. Only yesterday I told him I would not be buying anything more this month and asked him to make out our bill so that I could clear his account by the first. We already owe him hundred and eighty-three rupees. If we took another loan your guests will eat it up. They will go back merrily to their homes but what will we live on? You want us to eat at the free kitchen in the *gurdwara* all of the next month? New Year indeed! These fads are for the idle rich, people who frequent five-star hotels. We have barely enough to fill our bellies and never a *paisa* to spare. Only I know how I count every *paisa* to spread it out over thirty days!'

What was poor Kapoor to do? If you put your head in the jaws of a crocodile you cannot hope to escape without a scratch! He tried to explain in his softest tone: 'My good woman! This New Year is an English festival exactly like our *Baisakhi* or

Diwali.' But the good woman was beyond reasoning and refused to understand.

Exactly at quarter to eight the two men arrived accompanied by their wives and their brood of children. The women and children went into the inner room. Normally, children could be expected to create an uproar, but being clerks' offsprings they clung to their mothers's aprons and whimpered like little pups. In any case it was very cold evening, and their mothers could not get rid of them by ordering them to go out to play.

In the sitting-room the men were gathered around the bottle of Scotch. With it they nibbled salted peanuts. Inside, their women folk compared the prices of potatoes.

'In any event Kapoor Sahib owed us a feast for his promotion,' remarked Vashisht. Kapoor expanded like an inflated balloon. However, he pulled a long face and replied, 'What kind of promotion, *yaar!* Promotion is when there is an increase in one's salary. All I have got is increase of work. I used to get to the office at 10.30 in the morning and leave at 4:30 in the evening. Now I have to report at the Minister's residence at 7.45, and stay upto 8 or 9 p.m. I don't have to tell you all this.'

'To hell with the work, Mr Kapoor! Your sphere of influence has increased, your status risen to new heights!' remarked Gupta. 'Lots of things happen to people who occupy your chair. You recall that fellow called Sood? Narinder Sood was his full name. He used to sit in the same chair. It must have been about eight years ago when a licence applied for by a Bombay firm got stuck somewhere in the files of the Ministry. The firm's chaps had been going round and round for weeks but the Minister was like a duck which would not let a drop of water stay on its back. Utterly defeated, these Bombay Johnnies came to Sood's house and fell at his feet. This Sood fellow performed such jugglery that before the month was over, the licence was cleared. It was entirely Sood's handiwork. The Bombay people worked out that each visit to Delhi cost them five to six thousand rupees. So why not employ Sood to do the work for them? They persuaded him to resign his job and made him their Resident Executive Director in Delhi. They gave him an air-conditioned office and a spacious apartment. Now Mr. Sood and his pretty private secretary travel in a chauffeur-driven car. They make the rounds of different offices handing out invitation cards for dinner. He dines out every night with officials at swanky hotels like the Oberoi, the Taj or the Maurya. Every month lakhs of rupees pass through his hands; everyday he wears a new suit made of imported textiles.' Vashisht narrated the story of Sood's achievements as though they were blood-brothers.

'And *banda parwar* (protector of the poor) you must know that every currency note has a little glue stuck to it. As they are passed along from hand to hand some get stuck to one hand, some to another. You are a man of the world, you must know all this,' said Gupta.

Kapoor's third eye was beginning to catch a glimmer of light.

'My good friend, all I know is one basic fact. These eighty-four lakh species of lives that our holy books talk of are in fact one that of a clerk. A clerk goes through all the incarnations: cat, dog, scorpion, turtle, jackal, pig and everything else. And just as a person goes through the eighty-four lakhs of incarnations before he takes birth as a human to rule the world, so once in a millennia a clerk is fortunate enough to be appointed personal assistant to a minister.' Vashisht was well-versed in the holy texts.

'That may well be so,' conceded Kapoor with a half-hearted laugh, 'but there is no escaping from the fact that the work-load becomes much heavier. Your sister-in-law (my wife) has been going at me for the last ten days.'

'She is not sparing you!' sniggered Gupta.

'Why don't you put some sense in her head? Tell the good lady that by the grace of the chair you occupy all the four horizons will soon light up. Then she will cook *halva* full of dry fruits and glasses of milk laced with almonds before she sends to you to your office,' Vashisht roared happily.

'This bottle of Scotch is the first ritual — the sort of gift you give a bride when she first unveils her face,' added Gupta.

The two men treated Kapoor like a neophyte about to have its ears pierced before he is accepted by a Guru as his disciple. 'When my wife looked at this bottle, it seemed all hell would break loose,' said the new convert Kapoor.

Vashisht interrupted him by pleading in a mewling voice. 'Please, please explain all this to our *bhabhi*. Put some divine wisdom into her head.'

Gupta added his voice in support. Tell her how everyone in the Customs Service is eager to be posted at Palam or Santa Cruz airports and gets all sorts of influential people to speak for him. Every traffic constable, every sales tax officer does his level best to be posted in Chandni Chowk, Sadar or Chawri Bazar. How many shoes do they have to polish with butter before they get these postings? What is more, these big hospitals, when a doctor is put in charge of the wing reserved for VIPs his colleagues are burnt up with envy. Such posts do not go abegging. The work load is undoubtedly doubled. But just think: the bigger the head, the bigger the headache.'

'Now take the case of the Prime Minister,' said Vashisht, 'the poor thing works 18 to 19 hours everyday. During the elections the PM runs from one village to another. What booby prizes does the PM get for all this trouble?'

'Quite right! All these Ministers and leaders of political parties do not run around for the heck of it. Time will come when your wife will be singing and dancing with joy. She will take your big head in her lap and kiss away all its aches,' said Vashisht laughing.

The bottle was nearly empty. The peanuts had been nibbled away. Gupta glanced at his watch. 'Friends, it is nearly 9.30. Let us have something to eat. We will not get any buses after 10.30. And we are not ministers who can order our cars...' Kapoor got up and went inside. A little later Kapoor's children trooped in carrying bowls full of lentils cooked in onion and potato curry. The three men ate in the outer room; their wives and children in the room inside. Kapoor's wife was busy baking *chappaties*; her children ran around the two rooms serving them hot to the guests. By 10.15 the guests departed.

Kapoor felt like a criminal. He started making the beds in the rooms. He could hear his wife grumbling away as she rinsed the cooking pots and plates. 'New Year indeed! To hell with such festivals in this biting cold. They may suit white people. We have our own *Diwali* and *Baisakhi*, both in fair seasons. Only *Lohri* is in winter and people light bonfires to warm themselves. And I have to rinse all this garbage with icy cold water. To hell with this New Year.'

At long last the lights were switched off. The children were fast asleep. But Kapoor's wife went on nagging and grumbling. After a while she said: 'This New Year be damned! Why doesn't it fall on the 2nd of January? By then you will have drawn your salary.'

Kapoor kept silent.

His wife's voice flitted about in the dark like a bat going round and round the room. And then found a perch on some wall.

At the hour of midnight when lights in all the five-star hotels were dimmed so that men could embrace and kiss other men's wives and burst into singing *'auld lang syne'* to usher in the New Year, the Kapoors were fast asleep with their backs to each other.

164

One passenger ho!

Santokh Singh Dhir

Baroo, tonga-*wallah,* rose with the sun, harnessed his horse to the tonga and was the first to arrive at the stand outside the railway station. 'Anyone for Khanna?' he shouted, 'for Khanna, ho!'

Baroo knew that there was little chance of finding a passenger in the early hours of a winter morning. But nothing would daunt him. Even on frosty, winter mornings when his body shivered in the cold, his one thought was to be first at the tonga stand.

Baroo turned his face towards the bazaar and yelled at the top of his voice for a passenger — as if it was just one more he awaited. But not even that one he sought emerged from the bazaar. He turned towards the footpaths leading to different villages and called in the direction of each one. Not a sign of life! As if all the passengers of the world had been bitten by snakes. Baroo joined a hawker sitting by the side of the road and lit a *bidi.*

His horse showed signs of restlessness. It snorted a couple of times, swished its tail and took three steps on its own. 'Patience, Son! patience! Won't be long now! Let's wait for someone with a full purse and an empty brain and we'll be away.' Baroo leapt up, and tied the reins to the shaft.

The whistle of the train at the railway station pierced Baroo's ears like an arrow. He spat on the ground. He swore at the train and the man who had invented it. The express thundered by. And then the shuttle. 'It's these incestuous trains!' he cursed. 'One every hour,' and again he cried at the top of his voice for a passenger.

He lit another *bidi*. He inhaled strongly and in one long pull smoked away half of it. He exhaled through his nostrils, cursed the *bidi* and threw it away. The smoke burnt his mouth as if he had swallowed a handful of chillies.

The horse was restless. It stamped the earth with its hoofs; champed the bit between its teeth, shook the shafts of the tonga and the harness. The multi-coloured plume on its head fluttered in the air; the silk scarves tied to the bit waved like banners. A surge of pride went through Baroo's frame. 'Patience, brother! we'll soon be racing the wind...'

'Baroo, your horse is full of life; its always stamping its feet,' remarked the hawker.

'No horse like my horse!' exclaimed Baroo. 'Just look at the sheen of its coat! A fly would slither down if it alighted. I look after it as if it were my own son.'

'That's the only way to get the best out of an animal!' agreed the hawker.

The sun came up; but still no passenger for Khanna. More tongas came to the stand. And across the road Kundan was also calling for passengers for Khanna.

Baroo caught sight of a well-dressed man with a bag in his hand coming down the bazaar. Baroo watched his movements with a hawk's eye. The man came nearer the stand but gave no indication of where he was bound. The tonga*wallahs* began to shout.

'Come along here for Sirhind!' ...'Anyone for Maloh — O!' But the man betrayed no sign of his destination. When Baroo called for Khanna, the man did not as much as look up. 'These new-fangled gentlemen!' muttered Baroo to himself 'They're never in a hurry to open their mouths.'

The man stopped by Baroo's tonga and enquired in a barely audible voice, 'Have you any other passenger...?'

Baroo leapt down to take the man's bag and spoke most politely, 'Sir, you take the front seat... we'll leave in a jiffy — just take one more passenger.'

The man did not let go of his bag. What was the point of sitting in a tonga for an hour or more? He walked up to the front of the tonga and stopped near the footrest.

Baroo yelled as loud as he could for another passenger just one more passenger.

The man dumped his bag on the front seat and began to stroll around with his hands in his trouser pockets. Baroo patted his horse on the flanks and then began readjusting the rear seat. A cycle-rickshaw came and stopped by the tonga. The rickshawpuller struck a bargain with Baroo's passenger. Baroo's heart sank. '*Babuji,* there's strong head wind...' The cycle rickshaw won and bore its booty away.

The day was well-advanced.

Baroo went and sat by the hawker on the pavement. He had a strong urge to smoke his favourite brand of cigarette. But how could he squander two whole *pice* on a single cigarette? It looked like being a poor day. The rate was only four *annas* per passenger for Khanna; and there was a law against taking more than six. If he got only one load, it would be only one and a half rupees... it took three rupees every day to feed the horse. Why was he idling away his time on the pavement? He went and sat down on the rear seat of his tonga. Prospective travellers would feel that there was at least one passenger already present.

He began humming a film song and then a couplet out of *Heer Ranjha*. Then he stopped abruptly and peered at the fields at the distance. He espied a group of peasants coming along a footpath that coiled its way through the crops. In front were four rustics wrapped in black and white shawls. They looked as if bound for the law courts. Baroo turned his tonga towards them and shouted: 'Going to Khanna, Chaudhary? Let's be on our way.'

The peasants looked at each other. One of them spoke. 'We are bound for Khanna; but we will only go if you leave at once.'

'Certainly!' Baroo assured them. 'As soon as you are seated we'll be on our way.' Baroo grabbed the reins near the bit and turned his tonga towards the stand.

'We have to get to the *tehsildar's* court. We have a hearing at Samrala.'

'You get on the tonga. I'll get you there in a jiffy.' The men took their seats. Baroo turned towards the stand calling for just 'One more passenger'.

'Are you still looking for another?' asked one of the peasants. 'We should have known. A tonga*wala* is always a tonga*wala*.'

'Oh, let him make his living too,' replied another. 'It won't hurt us if we are a few seconds late.'

From the stand Baroo drove his tonga into the bazaar. He stood on the shaft and yelled, 'Anyone bound for Khanna — *baiee-o* one seat for Khanna.'

'You want to rob a lone passenger on the way?' shouted someone from the pavement. People began to laugh. Baroo bared his teeth in a grin showing his red gums. He joined in the laughter but continued calling for 'one passenger'. He parked his tonga on one side of the road leading to Khanna and rejoined the hawker.

'You are behaving exactly like other tonga*wallahs*,' complained one of the passengers.

'Brother tonga*wallah*, why do you harass us?' said another.

'We're not going to wait, Chaudhary! Just one more passenger. If he turns up, so much the better. If he does not, we'll go without him.'

Kundan noticed the agitation of Baroo's passenger. He took his tonga closer to Baroo's. 'I can take your passengers to Khanna...'

'Lay off, you son of a barber! Lay off your dirty ways!'

Baroo glowered at Kundan. He saw a cluster of women coming up. 'We'll be off now, Sardarji. There come more passengers.'

The peasants also saw the party of women and decided to wait a little longer.

The party came closer. Some of the women carried trays covered with tray cloths. The older women had veils drawn across their faces. The girls were in colouful costumes. Baroo stepped in front of the party and addressed them in a tone in which a dutiful son would address his mother. '*Maiji*, we were just waiting for you. Come along to Khanna'.

'No brother, we are on our way to the temple of the Mother-Goddess,' she replied casually.

'Yes, of course, *Maiji*,' said Baroo a little crestfallen.

'*Oi*, are you ever going to leave?' grumbled one of his party.

What an impatient lot passengers are!

Baroo had come to the end of his tether. He spoke candidly. 'It won't be long now. Just wait for one more passenger. Let me get my journey's worth.'

'While you count your costs, we'll have our case dismissed.'

Kundan chipped in again. 'Some people can be very simple and get caught in booby traps. This chap won't start; and if he does he'll never get you there. You'll find yourselves in a ditch. His horse is the wildest creature alive.'

Baroo turned pale with anger. He tried to keep his temper in control as he spoke to Kundan. 'Barber's son, is it the angel of death which makes you babble so? Go and get your Mama to oil your rickety cart; it creaks in every joint. And don't waste your time yapping like a pup.'

Kundan smacked his foot with his whip and called in an irritated tone: 'Come along all of you? I'll take three to Khanna on my chariot! I'll get you to Khanna in less than a minute... and for three *annas* only.' He edged his tonga forward.

Baroo's passengers were a little fed up. They didn't feel they were tied to him by any solemn contract. They began to dismount.

Baroo was in a rage. He called Kundan an incestuous raper of his mother. He tucked one end of his *tehmad* in his waist and challenged Kundan, 'Get off your trap, little boy.'

Baroo's temper unnerved Kundan. Nevertheless he dismounted. 'Mind your language, you bloody brewer!'

Baroo uttered another full-mouthed abuse and flourished his whip. 'You filthy fornicator of your sister! I'll pass you through the spokes of the wheel of my tonga.'

'I dare you to touch me!' Kundan kept a brave face despite his fright.

'Vanish, make yourself disappear, barber's son! I'll drink up your blood without letting a drop fall on the ground.'

Baroo only waited for Kundan to abuse him so that he could knock him down.

'What have I said to you that you should widen your nostrils in anger at me?' asked Kundan a little nervously.

'You steal my passengers.'

'I just call for passengers; you can tie up the ones you have.'

'I've been watching you since the morning; I'll tear up your top-knot by the roots.'

'You'll pull my top-knot will you?'

'You dare take over my passengers!'

'Come along *Babaji,*' said Kundan taking one of the peasants by the shoulder.

Baroo caught Kundan by the collar. Kundan grappled with him. The two began to wrestle. People rushed up to separate them. It took some time for the other tonga*wallahs* and the passengers to get the two apart. The contractor of the stand reprimanded them both soundly. Everyone was agreed that the passengers should go in Baroo's tonga. The passengers again took their seats.

People felt that he had had a raw deal and felt sorry for him; they wanted to get him the additional passenger and send him on his way. Even his passengers were willing to wait a little longer to let Baroo earn his full fare. All said and done, the poor chap had to fill his horse's belly before he could fill his own.

A head-constable of police came and enquired. 'Lads, any tonga leaving for Khanna?'

Baroo turned over the pros and cons in his mind. This chap wasn't going to pay a *pice;* but one could not say 'no' to a policeman. And with him there, he might put in two extra passengers. 'Come *Havildarji!* my tonga is ready to leave. Take the front seat.'

The Head-constable got on the tonga. Baroo called at the top of his voice for one more passenger.'

A shopkeeper came up from the bazaar and without a word got on Baroo's tonga. Two old women were coming up the road leading to the stand. Baroo called out to them, *'Mai*, you want to go to Khanna?' The women quickened their steps. One of them held up her hand, 'Hold on, brother!'

'Hurry up ladies,' exorted Baroo impatiently.

The women hurried up and clambered up the tonga. 'Brother, what will you be wanting?'

'Take your seats ladies. I won't fleece you!'

The tonga had eight passengers full-two rupees worth of fares. Perhaps the Lord would send along some more by the time he left and he might do a second trip. Baroo paid his tax to the contractor.

'I hope you won't look for more passengers now,' exclaimed one of the peasants.

'No Sirs, enough is enough. We'll take the name of the Lord and start.' Baroo patted his horse and untied the rope from the shafts.

He thought he might now buy himself a cigarette. He leapt off the tonga and went to the hawker to buy one of his favourite brand.

The Ambala-Ludhiana bus drew up beside the tonga. In a trice the passengers left the tonga and disappeared into the bus. The bus snorted like a dragon and vanished leaving clouds of diesel smoke and dust to settle on the tonga-drivers' faces.

Baroo stood in the centre of the stand, held up his whip and called with all his might: 'One seat for Khanna, *baiee o.*'

breaking point

Usha Mahajan

In the afternoons this corner of the restaurant was usually empty. By the evening the place filled up and it was futile coming there without a prior reservation in the hope of finding a place. That evening it appeared as if the whole of Calcutta had turned up for tea. Right from the elevators upto the entrance there was a queue waiting for tables and greedily eyeing those inside.

'I hope you haven't been waiting for too long!' he said as he sat down on the sofa and stretched his left leg to get his handkerchief out of his trouser pocket. 'There was heavy traffic all along the route. See, how I am sweating! And it's winter time.'

Madhukar wiped the beads of perspiration off his forehead. She fixed her gaze on him. He did not sound as if he was lying; he had a childlike innocence about him. She wanted to take the end of her sari and mop the pearls of sweat from his body.

'Why are you looking at me in this way?' he asked tenderly. He noticed her twisting the ends of her sari between her fingers. Gently he took her hand. The storm of emotions gathering within her found an outlet. Before she could check herself, the words burst out of her mouth, 'Madhukar, do you love me?'

He was taken aback almost as if his hand had touched a live wire or an icy blast of wind had blown into the easy corner of the restaurant and chilled the atmosphere. He suddenly let go her hand and sank back into his seat. 'The waiter is coming to take our order,' he replied and tried to look very business-like.

Madhukar's reluctance to answer a direct question made her very unsure of herself. How could she have been so brash as to expose herself so shamelessly before him? She felt as if a tidal wave of disillusionment had suddenly swept her off her feet and cast her on the hard rocks of reality. She realised she had blundered and felt sorry for herself. Married couples who have lived together for many years do not ever dare to ask each other such questions. What right had she to do so on the strength of just a few meetings?

Why did she have to bring up the question of love in their relationship? He was doing everything he could for her. He took her out for lunches and dinners to the most expensive joints in the city. And the countless little things he was always doing for her! Despite all that every time they met she looked into his eyes to find an answer to just one question.

Madhudar glanced at his wrist watch and said, 'Neera, I forgot about an appointment I made for four o'clock to see a patient in Ballygunge. It slipped out of my mind. Let's go; we'll come here another evening.' And without waiting for an answer, he got up and announced, 'I will drop you on the way.'

She followed him out of the restaurant feeling smaller and smaller till she felt reduced to a midget.

'Don't worry about me. It will make you go out of your way. I'll get home on my own,' she said trying hard to smile.

She spent the night thinking about him. She knew she should not see anymore of Madhukar; but she also knew she would not be able to keep up her resolve. The more she tried to put him out of her mind, the stronger became her desire to win over Madhukar's heart. The next evening when Madhukar dropped in on the excuse of seeing her sick husband, she felt she had got a second lease of life. He brought him a bouquet of flowers; she knew that it was really meant for her because they were her favourite gladioli. He knew she kept them in her vase till the last blossom had withered away.

As she was leaving, he touched her lightly on her shoulders and murmured, 'Sorry about last evening.'

Neera could not make out what he was apologising about for — not having replied to her question or not having given her tea. However, she felt there must be something abiding in their relationship to make him come to see her. Maybe soon the time would come when she could put him the same question and he would answer, 'Yes.'

All said and done, what else is it that keeps humans alive except hope. It was the same with her husband. He had been badly injured in a traffic accident but had hung on to life in the hope that he would be his old self again.

She remembered how lying in bed in the hospital, he had said, 'Neera, I don't think I will be of any use to you any longer. Would you like to be freed of me?'

She had broken down. She had run her trembling fingers across the face of the man who had been her life's support but was now lying disabled and helpless. She reassured him, 'Don't ever say such things again. I'll never leave you. I wish God had inflicted this injury on me rather than on you.'

Time takes its toll of everything. It not only ages the face and the body but the head and the heart as well. Time makes people forget their own worlds, forget the solemnity of vows made. When rains fall, withered trees begin to sprout fresh leaves. The scorching sun of midsummer turns the same green woodland into a barren desert. There was time when she had

175

waited anxiously all day for the evening when her husband would be back home. And now that he was home all day long, she felt that there was nothing left in the world for her to look forward to.

How could she ever forget what Madhukar had done for her! When her world had become pitch-dark without a glimmer of hope anywhere, he had taken her out into the light. He had assuaged the pain that she had inflicted upon herself through self-torture. She had become a living corpse; he had breathed life back into her.

'Look upon me as a friend. Tell me all that you have on your mind. Grief shared is a burden lightened,' Madhukar had said to solace her.

Alas! if only anguish in the heart could be lessened by opening it out to others! Inner sorrow is an unending, wordless tale which only the truly concerned can comprehend.

At the time she felt that no one could read her mind better than Madhukar. She started adorning her days and nights with the pearls of dreams surrounding him. In her desert she saw a mirage of sparkling, life-giving water. Never before in her life had she felt herself closer to anyone as she felt to Madhukar.

The last five years had not been without meaning for them. They had gone a long way together. He set the pace, holding her hand in a tight grasp to help her keep up with him. His name was now listed amongst the most successful doctors in the city. He never had any problem with money; now he had plenty to squander. He could not bear to see Neera living in a miserable, dilapidated tenement in Tollygunj. He bought her a spacious apartment in Calcutta's upper class south district and made special arrangements for her husband's treatment. The same Madhukar who had shied away on hearing the word 'love' had showered her with affection. He had also seen how devoted Neera was to him. She catered to every little whim that took his fancy; in his hands she was like a puppet dancing to his tune. All this was concrete proof, if any were needed, that in his happiness she found fulfilment.

There was only one problem. Her seven-year-old son, Anjul, had taken a dislike to 'Uncle' Madhukar. 'Mama, you should not leave Papa alone and go out with uncle,' he had often grumbled. It was Madhukar who had suggested that Anjul be put in a boarding school in Darjeeling. It would make a man out of him. His own son was in the same boarding school. Her heart swelled with pride at his concern with her problems. He looked upon her son as if he was his own child. Why else would he want to give him the same opportunties as he was providing his own son? How she had cried when time came for Anjul to leave home. She had steeled her heart and agreed to Madhukar's proposal because she believed that it would be best for her son to stay away from her.

Receiving favours can become such a burden that there comes a time when one is better off freed of them. However, her husband had fallen in line with all that had happened. But the burden of favours received was borne by her. It had become a habit. But even with her the load was becoming too heavy for her shoulders. She felt like throwing it off and casting it into a gutter. Thereafter, she could not care what slights and kicks she got from the passersby. Perhaps it was this kind of fate that her husband had wanted to save her from.

That day had been really dreadful. Madhukar had dropped her home. The lift was out of order. She ran out of breath climbing the long flights of stairs. She had barely turned the key to let herself in when she heard him call, 'Neera, come here.' It had been ages since he had called by her name; most of the time it was 'anyone there?' An unknown fear gripped her heart. He was helpless paralytic — what could he possibly do to her? Even so, she could not muster up courage to face him. She came upto the door of his room and noticed a strange gleam of resignation in his eyes. 'Come to me, Neera.' The voice was full of life. She went and sat down on the corner of his bed. He picked up his son's photograph from the side-table and began to stare at it. 'Neera, will you agree to do what I ask of you?' Before she could reply he said, 'Get Anjul to come back home. Let him stay with you.' Then after a pause he said in a flat monotone, 'Neera, why don't you marry Madhukar? He loves you. You can forget all about me.'

She felt the earth slip away from under her feet. She did not dare to raise her eyes to meet his. 'I'll get your paper,' she said and went to the kitchen.

Marry? What on earth for? Is marriage the ultimate of all man-woman relationships? Is marriage all that holds them together? If there is more to it, what is it? Despite being married, Madhukar had come to her to steal a few moments of happiness. Was the bright vermilion she wore in the parting of her hair just a symbol of her belonging to her disabled husband? What was it that Madhukar had not done for her? He came to see her because he preferred her company to that of his wife. Would not asking for more amount to asking for too much? An admission of pettiness and greed? Of wanting to displace his wife and children to make room for herself? Shame on her! How could she ever think of doing such a thing! Admittedly she had often dreamt of appearing openly in society with Madhukar's hand in hers; but dreaming it was and no more. Wasn't she paying the price for being 'the other woman'? Another name for love is sacrifice.

She heard the sound of something crashing and the splintering of glass. Perhaps Anjul's framed photograph had fallen down. She took the platter of food and hurried to her husband's bedside. Her hands began to shake. Anjul's picture was lying on the floor; her husband's left arm was dangling by the bed; a deathly pallor had spread over his face; his lifeless eyes carried an accusation of guilt. Was it for this that he had summoned her to his bedside? Something inside her snapped and opened a flood-gate of pent-up emotions. She felt as if she had cut a limb of her own body and thrown it away.

The neighbours heard her screams and came running in. She could not recall how she passed that night. She tried to send word to Madhukar. There was not a trace of him. Her neighbours helped her to arrange all the details of the funeral.

For the first time it occurred to her how secure she had felt with that helpless, invalid husband of hers. How could she bear to live alone now? If only Madhukar had come over, taken her in his arms and said, 'Neera, what makes you think you have been left alone? I will always be with you. You are not a widow; I am your protector and your husband.'

She got up and faced the mirror. Her eyes were swollen with crying and wailing. Her hair was dishevelled; the *bindi* mark was spattered across her forehead. She refused to wipe it off. For the last many years, she had put it there to please Madhukar. She took a little vermilion powder from her box and with a trembling finger put the *bindi* mark where it always had been.

She could no longer control herself. With fear in her heart she rang up Madhukar's home. She had never dared to do this before. It was Madhukar's wife who picked up the receiver.

'This is Neera calling. Can I speak to Madhukar? Its very urgent.'

After a pause a very acid voice replied, 'Aren't you satisfied with all that you have grabbed? Or do you now want to break into my home as well? For God's sake leave me alone.' The receiver was put down.

A storm of anger welled up in her mind. Surely she had a claim on everything connected with Madhukar. From the time they had got to know each other, she had hung on every breath he took. If his wife had been so conscious of safeguarding her 'wife's rights,' why wasn't she able to keep him tied down with bonds of love? For the first time Neera realised the existence of Madhukar's wife and sensed her own helplessness. The question of status suddenly arose in her mind.

The next evening Madhukar came to see her. She wanted to run up to him, put her head against his broad chest and cry her heart out till she had shed all her tears. Why she remained rooted to the spot she did not know; nor why Madhukar had that uncertain look in his eyes. It seemed as if he wanted to say something but could not find the exact words.

Ultimately, Neera broke the silence, 'Where were you?'

'I was out of town. I had to leave suddenly. I would have come over as soon as I was back. But you rang up for me at home — I don't know why. My wife was very upset and created a scene. To avoid it getting worse I kept away yesterday.'

'He could not come because...'

Something very tender preserved with care and patience over the years had suddenly snapped. The web of illusions that she had spun out of the threads of hope had come apart. Was this the moment of truth for which she had waited so long and for which she had defied all social conventions and given herself body and soul to Madhukar?

A heavy silence descended on the room; a pall of gloom darker than when her husband had died, enveloped her. Tears welled up in her eyes and fell on her wrists. She turned her face towards the window. The sun was about to set. In the dim light of the heavily curtained room, Madhukar was unable to see another sun setting in Neera's tear-sodden eyes and another hearse wading through them.

She drew one end of her sari and rubbed the bindi off her forehead, smashed her bangles against the arms of the chair and was convulsed with hysterical sobbing. Madhukar could not make out what had come over her. Between the splintered glass of bangles were drops of blood. Madhukar tried to comfort her. 'Neera, take a hold on yourself. Things will soon take a turn for one better. See you have cut your wrists.' He ran and got out his first-aid kit.

She cried and cried till she could cry no more. Madhukar sat by her for a long time trying to make out what had happened to her. As he left he said, 'Neera, take a little rest. You are not yourself today. I'll look again tomorrow.'

She had a blank look in her wide open eyes. She did not turn round to see him leave.

He came the next day. He knocked at her door many times. All he could hear was sound of sobbing. The door did not open. He turned back grumbling to himself, 'She is still mourning her dead husband. Perhaps she loved him.'

Strange new world

Kulwant Singh Virk

How Hazara Singh made a comfortable living without putting his hand to tilling or any other conventional mode of occupation was a mystery to many in the village. But those who knew, never tired of admiring his unusual skill at cattle-lifting or house-breaking and of relating stories of his nightly adventures.

In children's story books, thieves generally end up locked behind impregnable prison bars. But Hazara Singh had never been to jail. In fact, he was not even among those acknowledged miscreants whom the police inspector, on his occasional visits to the village, would summon and openly beat up in our school compound, by way of routine chastisement.

The visit of the Inspector, who always camped in our school, meant a holiday for us. But we did not stir out of doors for fear of policemen. We only listened, all agog, from the roofs of our houses, to the yells and cries of the criminals, coming from the school campus.

On such occasions, Hazara Singh, in his immaculate white turban, sat with the police dignitary on the string charpoy, talking to him; or he would be seen busily running around making arrangements for the officer's board and stay.

Whatever little land Hazara Singh possessed was cultivated by his tenants and he seemed to lead a life unburdened with any visible care or responsibility. Other peasants clad themselves in coarse home-spun and could only afford, on rare festive occasions, to wear clothes bought from town. Hazara Singh always wound round his head a respectable length of fine muslin and had ample yardage of mill-made white calico loosely draped round his waist.

Apparelled opulently in this guise, Hazara Singh would frequently be seen visiting his friends or relations in the neighbouring villages. In his own village he sat among the elders and was always the central figure in such assemblies. He could talk of various things delightfully and was full of anecdotes and stories, with which he held his listeners entranced.

I loved hearing Hazara Singh talk, especially of his daring exploits. Whenever I was home on holiday from my school in town, I spent long hours listening to his tales told with humour and descriptive skill. He was evidently proud of his prowess at cattle-lifting and at house-breaking, but from his narration it was not difficult to guess that he relished the former procedure more than the latter. It gave him a greater sense of triumph. It was, to him, like winning over troops from the enemy ranks. Whenever we sat together, Hazara Singh would lapse into a reminiscent mood.

'One day my nephew came to me,' he recounted once, sitting upon a tree-stump and scratching the earth with a twig, 'and said that he needed a pair of bullocks. He had seen one pair belonging to the Chathas of Ajnianwala and wanted me somehow to deliver this to him at his farm! I told him that the Chathas were his father's friends and that he would not be able to keep their bullocks if they discovered where they were. And if he was ultimately going to have to return the animals, why must he expose me to the rigours of cold wintry nights? But he was insistent and assured me that I could count upon his ability to retain the animals once I managed to pass them on to him. I promised I would.

'It was no easy task unfastening those animals. It was the finest pair — and the cleverest I ever encountered. They would start at the slightest semblance of a shadow, and once frightened it was very difficult to lay hold of them. Round their necks they wore rows of noisy trinkets which raised a loud alarm.

'I had of course taken with me two handfuls of green fodder. Sniffing food in my lap, the animals, instead of getting frightened, stretched out their heads towards me. Caressing them affectionately with my fingers, I took off the trinkets from their necks and walked out quietly with the two animals following me. The pair was well known in that part of the country and anybody within a radius of nine or ten miles would at once have recognised it. I had taken with me a fast mare and rode off with the bullocks strung to the saddle — really good oxen will always follow a galloping horse! With the rise of the sun next morning I had done more than twenty miles and we reached the village of Ranike to greet my cousins — sons of my mother's sister — with an early, "Good morning." I tied the animals in their sugar-cane farm and lay down on a charpoy to rest in the sun. By nightfall again I set out with the animals and arrived at my nephew's farm before daybreak.

'The owners had been following close upon my heels. It was not difficult to keep track of three fleeing animals. Next day they also reached there. They knew for certain where their bullocks were and brought batches of common friends to intercede in their behalf. My nephew at last gave in and returned the animals. I still rag him about it; he has no answer when I ask him why he made me ride through those two chilly nights if he could not keep the bullocks.'

Animal-lifting was interesting, but there was a great deal more money in house-breaking and Hazara Singh was no less proficient at it. His first principle in the technique of house-breaking was, 'Avoid all noise at all costs!' and he had ready-made formulae to this end. 'Cloth' he would say, 'is the best absorbent of sound. Cover up with cloth all those objects that are likely to make a sound.'

The neighbouring villages he had classified into two distinct categories — 'his own' villages where he would never dream of doing anything and 'others', where he could operate freely without any qualms. But it was difficult to say which set of villages was dearer to him. He knew all these so well; their roads and pathways, bushes and pastures, canals and streamlets, he knew them all intimately. Even as a bee flitting from one flower to another, drinking the honey, considers the whole garden her own, or as a youth visiting his maternal village regards all homes with equal affection. Hazara Singh loved all these villages, whether 'his own' or 'others.' Hazara Singh was proud of the art he possessed and he made no secret of it. Not many people he would say, were so fleet of hand and foot.

'The money-lenders of Mangewala had a *pucca* built house,' he told us once. The outer walls were plastered over with cement and were thought to be invulnerable. One day I heard the money-lenders had come into a good bit of crisp money in lieu of mortgaged land they had released. Now this was a wonderful opportunity.

'Four of us set to work. There were four men sleeping in the front of the house, completely oblivious of the back rooms. I knew it was not easy to break through the walls and decided to cut into the foundation under the wall. We kept digging away until the small hours of the morning and managed to worm a tunnel into the house below the wall. Collecting whatever we could lay our hands on we made good our escape. Next day the police inspector came and visited the spot. I was also present. As he went in and came out through the tunnel again, he praised the man responsible, and admired his ingenuity and hard toil. He said he would compliment him,' Hazara Singh chuckled, when he was caught!'

House-breaking was a sport for him — a sport which was exciting to him for its risks. But he would always give a different impression to his friends. 'This is no joke really,' he would say solemnly. 'You never know for a moment if you will be able to get away by the path you entered by. Of course, I think nothing of encountering three or four persons, for I can run and can also wield a stick as well as anyone. But it is always a hare-and-hounds affair you know. Once three of us entered a village under cover of darkness. Two of us started cutting through a wall while the third stood on watch round the corner. He dozed off, the wretch, but we unknowing, carried on with our work relying on him to warn us if anything went amiss. Meanwhile, someone in the village saw us and went around collecting men. As I was creeping into the passage we had carved out, I heard dogs bark. I asked my companion to wait. Next moment I saw a crowd of people barring the street whence we had entered. They thought that was the only way of escape open to us. I calculated differently. Instead of backing out into the street we went into the house, jumped over the wall into another house and, thus repeating the process a few times, escaped out of harm's way.

'Later the villagers came to know of it and whenever we met they would chaff me. "So, you nearly robbed our Shah!" "It is all a matter of luck," I would reply, "I don't know what you would have done to me had I been caught." All a question of chance.'

Then came the Partition and the land of the five waters was torn in two. Hazara Singh leaving the villages he had so loved, the farms and fields canals and highways of which he knew every square inch, trudged his weary way with a caravan of refugees over the border to Karnal. This too was Punjab he was told, and here too there were villages and houses, farms and canals. But everything seemed so different to him! How could this environment, so strange and uninspired, ever be 'home'? thought Hazara Singh.

After a few weeks I also arrived there. I had been looking forward to meeting Hazara Singh. He appeared to me the only stable element in that changing, crumbling world. He, surely, would be unaltered, still skilled and adventurous. I was wrong. Hazara Singh too, like all of us, was uprooted and lost.

'It hardly makes a difference to you, uncle,' I said to him one day with the brashness of youth. 'Like government officials you are just the same here as you were there, aren't you?'

'How can that be, son?' asked Hazara Singh quietly. 'How am I different from my brothers? Am I not a sharer in their sorrows and trials?'

'That is true; but if one possesses an art like yours, one can surely cash in on it anywhere, can't one?'

'Oh, you mean that! Well, no; no, indeed. Far, far from it.' Hazara Singh shook his head sadly. 'My steps waver upon this ground. How can I do anything here? One needs the sights and sounds of home, the faces of friends and kinsmen. Here,' he repeated, 'I can do nothing.'

Neither danger nor fear of the law had ever balked Hazara Singh, but a strange new world defeated him.

a punjab pastorale

Khushwant Singh

Peter Hansen was a young American from Illinois. His father was a Swede who had settled in the United States and made good as a stockbroker. Peter was given the best an American youth could desire in the way of schooling and university education, and in due course joined his father's firm. It did not take him long to discover that he was not meant for business. His spirit of adventure felt cramped in horizons clogged with skyscrapers. He yearned for the wide open spaces and wanted to serve humanity. He gave up stockbroking and took to Christianity, left Illinois and came to India. His Mission ordered him to preach the gospel of Christ among the Sikh peasantry in Punjab. This brought Peter Hansen to Amritsar.

Hansen plunged into the humanitarian business with American thoroughness. He drew up maps of the countryside and stuck little flags to mark the villages he would visit. He made lists in an indexed register, of villagers he had to contact, together with details of their private lives. He bought an American army motorcycle, and within a few weeks of his arrival Padre Hansen and his *phut-phut* became a familiar sight in the district.

Hansen was a missionary, but with a difference. He did not go about peddling religion. It was reform he was after —

social reform, economic reform, educational reform, moral reform. His method too was different. He did not believe in preaching or proselytising but in reform by example and personal contact.

'Once you get to know them,' he used to say, 'you can make them do anything.'

Hansen and I were destined to meet. I, too, had a heart for humanity, only I did nothing about it except talk. But Hansen did not know that. I was not religious and had taken to Marxism. Even that did not bother Hansen, he was a bit of a Socialist himself. He happened to attend a meeting I was addressing.

'The country is ripe for revolution,' I was saying. 'It needs proper leadership to get it going. High falutin talk of dialectical materialism and Marxist economics does not register on the rural mind. We must preach Socialism through example and personal contact. We must denounce police oppression, corruption and injustice in the law courts. Above all, we must get to know the people. Once you get to know them — you can make them do anything.'

Hansen and I shook hands and a partnership to further the cause of progress was made.

One hot May morning we decided to give our enterprise a trial. Hansen rigged himself out in his touring clothes — a white jockey cap, a tight-fitting vest, a pair of very short shorts and sandals on his feet. I donned my socialist garments of the coarsest handspun *khaddar,* mounted Hansen's motorcycle pillion and we shot out of Amritsar.

Some fifteen miles east of the city, there was a big canal which ran at right angles to the road. We crossed the bridge and turned off the metal road onto a cart-track. The track showed visible signs of wear and tear. Bullock-cart wheels had left deep ruts which ran criss-cross like intersecting tram lines. Hansen did not seem to notice them. He sped on with a grim resolve, his belly hugging the petrol tank. I held stoically on to his vest. I could find no protruding gadgets on which to rest my feet, and they dangled helpless above the hot exhaust pipes. I did not dare to protest. There were greater things in offing, and I could not go down just because the going was rough. But I did go down. While Hansen's eyes were glued to the distant horizon as if straining to get a glimpse of the domes of Shangrila, we flew over a ditch at some forty miles per hour. I was tossed in the air and by the time I came down Hansen and his motorcycle were several yards ahead on their philanthropic errand. I landed in the middle of a very dusty track. It didn't hurt much, but it was somewhat undignified. My turban had flown off and my long hair spread clumsily over my face. Hansen pulled up and looked concerned for a moment. Then he flashed his teeth at me like a cheap toothpaste advertisement and burst out laughing.

'You look too darned funny for words,' he roared. 'Just as well it happened here. This is where we break off. Soorajpur is just across those fields, behind the *keekar* trees.' Hansen ran his motorcyle down the canal bank to a large *peepul* tree, still laughing. I collected my scattered belongings and joined him. I opened his water bottle, poured the water down my parched throat and splashed it on my dusty face. Then I stretched myself in the welcome shade of the *peepul,* and was at peace with my surroundings.

Soorajpur was just visible through the thick cluster of *keekar* trees. All around it stretched a vast expanse of wheat fields. The corn was ripe and ready for harvesting. A soft breeze blew across the golden cornfields like ripples over a lake. Under the trees the cattle and the cow-herds lay in deep slumber. It was a scene typical of pastoral Punjab on a summer afternoon.

It was too peaceful to think of revolution. My enthusiasm was somewhat on the wane. I was willing to leave Soorajpur to its slovenly backwardness.

But Hansen's ardour had not cooled. Just as I had shut my eyes in peaceful contemplation, he started to talk.

'The last time I was here there was a crisis going on. The Sikhs would not let the Christians into their temple because the Christians were sweepers and skinned dead buffaloes.'

'Oh?' I enquired politely, 'what happened?'

'I told the Christians to go and tell the Sikhs that they would give up skinning dead buffaloes if they were allowed in the temple. Just then a buffalo died right near the most popular village well and no one would touch it. The place was full of crows and vultures and the stink was terrible. I got round Moola Singh — you must meet the old man — and told him to persuade the Sikhs to think over the matter. He told his fellow Sikhs to remove the carcass themselves or let the Christians into the temple. Sure as ever, they came round. Now the Christians are paid twenty rupees for skinning a dead buffalo. They sell the hide for another thirty or forty rupees, and they walk in and out of the Sikh temple as they please. It was all really because of Moola Singh. Personal contact does so much. I've always said once you get to know these village folk you can make them do anything. And Moola Singh is a grand old fellow. Come along, we had better be moving.'

And so we started off again. This time Hansen was on the motorcyle, and I was pushing it across ploughed fields and dry water courses. Hansen was apparently very popular. Everyone who saw him came around to greet him. He knew the names of all of them. In the traditional fashion, he shook them by both hands and put his hands across his heart. No one took any notice of me nor volunteered to help me push the motorcyle.

I pushed hand-shaking Hansen and his motorcyle up a narrow alley to the centre of the village. We parked the machine by a well amid a crowd of urchins and proceeded to Moola Singh's house, which was a few metres away. Moola Singh was to be my first contact and I was to deliver to him all my Socialism. At night I was to address a meeting at the temple with Moola Singh to back me up. Hansen would visit the house of the Christians who lived on the outskirts of the village.

We caught Moola Singh unawares. Hansen's enquiries about him had evinced no answer from the crowd walking along with us towards his courtyard. When we got to his house, we saw his two wives sitting under the shadow of a wall. One was rubbing clarified butter into the head of the other. They too were reticent about Moola Singh. Suddenly becoming aware of this mysterious silence, Hansen turned to the crowd and asked the reason for it. They all looked at each other but no one would answer. Then all of a sudden appeared Moola Singh on his threshold. He was a large hulking man over six feet in height. His hair hung over his shoulders and mingled with his beard. He was about sixty, but a youthful roguish smile played about his face.

He stretched his arms wide and gathered Hansen in a friendly embrace. Through the mass of hair and beard I heard Hansen calling out my name. Moola Singh held out one hand to me, still holding the American by the other. He clasped him again and the two swayed in a close, amorous embrace. Moola Singh was stinking of drink. Saliva dribbled from his mouth onto his shaggy beard. It ran down like threads of silver on Hansen's hazel-brown hair. Hansen winced as the liquid ran through his hair onto his scalp. With a little jerk he extricated himself from Moola Singh's grasp and pushed him back gently.

Hansen was too well bred to lose his temper. He smiled his toothpaste advertisement smile and poked Moola Singh in the ribs.

'Bahut sharab! Bahut sharab!' he rebuked in Hindustani.

Moola Singh grinned. He caught both his ears with his hands and stuck out his yellow tongue in a gesture of repentance.

'Never again, Sahib. This is the last time — *toba, toba.* You come to my house and I am stupidly drunk. If you forgive me this time and promise to come again, I will not touch drink any more.'

Hansen forgave him and promised to come again. We left Moola Singh's house a little depressed. I began to think that our ardour for reform was somewhat adolescent. Hansen was wiping the dribble off his hair with his handkerchief and cursing the Sikhs. The Christians folk, he insisted, were so much nicer. They didn't drink. They didn't grow long hair and beards which stank of sweat and stale clarified butter. Since he had got to know them, they were living a clear Christian life — free of pagan superstition which beset the life of the hirsute Sikh. He dismissed the crowd with a firm wave of the hand and we walked down to the mission school.

We entered the Christian habitation with more optimism. Mr. Yoosuf Masih, the teacher, welcomed us and put a garland of marigolds around Hansen's neck. Sweeper women and children gathered about him in a chorus of *salaams.* Hansen patted the children and shook hands with their mothers. So much cleaner than the Sikhs, he said with a triumphant smile. He insisted on my going inside their huts and seeing for myself. The first hut had a large picture of the black, red-tongued, multi-armed goddess Kali hanging in the centre of a wall. Others also had pictures. In fact, we saw the entire Hindu pantheon: Shiva on his tiger skin with serpents twining around his neck; Ganesha riding the mouse, his lady love seated on his elephantine thigh; Saraswati standing in spotless white on a large lotus. Hansen saw them too. I smiled at him but he looked away. He shook hands with Mr. Yoosuf Masih rather abruptly, promising to see him later in the evening. We then made our way back towards the village well to our motorcyle.

We walked a long way without speaking. Hansen was somewhat depressed. I was just bored and tired. As we approached the well, Hansen spoke.

'Queer country this! You do not know where to start. When you've begun, you are not sure if you are going about it the right way. When you look back to see how far you've got, you find that you've got nowhere. It's like a stream losing itself in the desert sand. It dries up so quickly that you cannot even find its traces.' I made no comment.

The sun went down and the shades of twilight gathered Soorajpur in their fold. The moon was in the first quarter and shed a soft, silky light in the narrow alleys. Hansen started talking again. If only Christian converts would free themselves from the clutches of superstition. If only Sikhs would give up dissipating and use their fine manhood towards something constructive. If...if...if...The burden of the world's woes seemed to have descended on him and he looked miserable and woebegone.

Suddenly Hansen stopped talking. He sat up straight as if electrified. From Moola Singh's courtyard emerged a girl, barely sixteen, with two pitchers balanced on her stately head. She came towards the well where we were sitting. She wore a man's striped shirt. It had no buttons in the front and made a V formation running from her neck down to the middle of her flat belly. On either side, the V was misshaped by her youthful breasts. Hansen's eyes were fixed on her. His mouth was wide open. The girl drew several buckets of water from the well and we watched. The depression lifted, and the streets of slovenly Soorajpur were charged with romance and mellowed moonlight. The girl went with the two pitchers balanced on her head. Her slim figure disappeared into Moola Singh's courtyard.

Hansen came back to earth. 'Oh my, oh my, that was sum'pn. She is old Moola Singh's daughter. Hardly believe it, would you? She is like a flower in the desert, and desert flowers always smell sweeter. They have to make up for the desert. I could almost write a poem about her.'

We sat by the well for a long time, feeling strangely happy. Hansen was trying hard to give his emotions a poetical form. 'I've got it,' he exclaimed, snapping his fingers and looking up at the sky —

'She walks in beauty like the night.'

notes on the authors

1. AJEET CAUR: (1934-) She is one of the better known Punjabi writers. Some of her important collection of short stories are *Gulbano, Mahik Di Maut, But Shikan, Saviyan* and *Churiyan.* And among her novelettes are *Postmortem, Dhup Wala Sheher, Khana Badosh* and *Kachche Ranga De Sheher.* She is the recipient of Punjabi Academy Award, 1984 and Sahitya Academy Award, 1986 for *Khana Badosh.*

2. AMRITA PRITAM: (1919-2005) Widely acknowledged as the doyen of Punjabi litterateurs, she was a distinguished Punjabi poet and a writer with more than 70 published books to her credit. *Kagaz Te Canvas* (poetry), *Pinjar* (novel), *Yatri* (novel), *Ih Sach Hai* (novel), *Kore Kagaz* (novel) are some of her famous works. Her autobiography *Rasidi Tikat* received rave reviews. *Kagaz Te Canvas* earned her the covetous Jnanpith Award for 1982. She received !he Sahitya Academy Award in 1956. She held D. Litt. of four Indian Universities. Her works have been translated into 34 Indian and foreign languages.

3. BALWANT GARGI: (1916-2003) He was a Punjabi playwright, a director and a film maker. He founded the Department of Indian Theatre at the Punjab University. His first play *Loha Kut* published in 1944 established him as a popular playwright. His powerful dramas include *Kwari Teesi, Dhooni Di Agg, Sultan Razia* and *Nimm De Pattee.* His controversial autobiography *The Naked Triangle* propelled him to the forefront of the Indian literary and cultural scene. He was

awarded the Sahitya Academy Award in 1962 and the Padma Shri in 1973.

4. BALWANT SINGH: (1926-) A Punjabi creative writer who has published *Rat, Chor Aur Chand* (novels), *Punjab Ki Kahaniah* (short stories), *Jagga* (stories and plays).

5. GULZAR SINGH SANDHU: (1935-) He is a journalist by profession. His literary and creative writings include a translation of *Tess of the D'Urbervilles* into Punjabi and *Sade Har Shringar* (a novel).

6. GURMUKH SINGH JEET: (1922-) Apart from being a widely respected critic of Punjabi literature, he is an author equally at ease in Punjabi and Hindi. Amongst his better known works are *Kaala Aadmi, Dharti Son Sunehari, Mrig Trishna, Vekho Kaun Aaye* (all in Punjabi) and *Thandi Deewaren, Shikhar Aur Shunya* and *Ek Din Ka Sultan* (in Hindi). He has also been a member of the Executive Board of Punjabi Sahitya Academy.

7. KARTAR SINGH DUGGAL: (1917-) He writes both in Urdu and Punjabi and has published 21 collections of short stories, eight novels, seven full-length plays and two collections of poems. He received the Sahitya Academy Award in 1965 and the Soviet Land Nehru Award in 1981. He was honoured by Delhi Administration as a distinguished Punjabi Litterateur in 1976 and was awarded the Padma Bhushan in 1988. In addition to his literary contribution, he has served with distinction as Station Director of All India Radio and as Director of the National Book Trust.

8. KHWAJA AHMED ABBAS: (1914-1989) He was a journalist, novelist and a film producer-director of international repute. A writer with leftist leanings, he published over 40 books in Urdu including *Diya Jale Sari Raat* (novel), *Main Kaun Hun, Ek Ladki* and *Zafran Ke Phul* (all collections of short stories). His other important works include *When Night Falls, Face to Face with Khrushchev,* a 2-part biography of Mrs. Indira Gandhi — *Indira Gandhi: Return of the Red Rose* and its sequel *That Woman.*

9. KISHEN SINGH DHODI: This is his first story to be translated into English. He has also written other Punjabi short stories. He runs a motor business in Delhi.

10. KRISHEN CHANDER: (1914-1977) Widely acclaimed as one of the finest short story writers in Urdu after Premchand, Krishen Chander reached the height of his fame with *Ek Gadhe Ki Sarguzasht (Autobiography of a Donkey)*, published in 1957 which sold over 2,00,000 copies. His works, which comprised nearly 80 volumes, covered a wide range of themes. His works reflected his protest against exploitation of man by man and showed deep sympathy and understanding of the suffering of the downtrodden. His concern for humanity ran through his stories *Hum Vaishi Hain, Kalu Bhangi, Mahalakshmi Bridge, Tai Eesri, Nai Ghulami* and *Jab Khat Jage*. His books have been translated into many Indian, European and Chinese languages.

11. KULWANT SINGH VIRK: (1920-   ) A journalist and a Punjabi creative writer, he has been the Joint Director, Communication Centre, Punjab Agriculture University, Ludhiana. He wrote six volumes of short stories in Punjabi: *Chhah Wela*, 1950; *Dharti Te Akash*, 1951; *Tun Di Paud*, 1954; *Dudh Da Chhapper*, 1958; *Gohlan*, 1961 and *Naven Lok*, 1968. He received The Sahitya Academy Award for *Naven Lok* in 1968.

12. RAJINDER SINGH BEDI: (1915-1984) Starting his career as a clerk in the Postal Department he rose to become Station Director, AIR, Jammu in 1948. Then he took to writing and making films. As a powerful Urdu writer he published novels *Ek Chadar Maili Si* in 1962, *Apna Dukh Mujhe De Do* in 1965; short stories *Dana 0 Dam*, 1938, *Grehan*, 1941 and *Haath Hamare Kalam Hue*, 1974; and plays *Bejan Chizen*, 1943, *Sat Khel*, 1981. He was awarded the Sahitya Academy Award for *Ek Chadar Maili Si* in 1965.

13. SAADAT HASAN MANTO: (1912-1955) He is widely regarded as one of the best Urdu writers. In a literary and journalistic

career spanning more than two decades, he wrote over 200 stories, apart from plays, film scripts, novels and essays. *Toba Tek Singh, Mozail* and *Mummy* are some of his powerful stories. He lived in Amritsar, Bombay and Lahore.

14. SANTOKH SINGH DHIR: (1922-   ) He is a journalist and a Punjabi creative writer. *Gudian Patole* and *Poh Phutala* (both poetry) are among his important published works.

15. SATINDRA SINGH: (1924-   ) He is a political journalist and a short story writer. *Muk Di Gal* is his published collection of short stories.

16. UPENDRA NATH ASHK: (1910-1996) He began his career as a radio and a print journalist before he took to creative writing. He wrote more than 75 books, including 12 novels, 13 full length plays and 13 collection of short stories. He wrote in both Hindi and Urdu. Some of his important works include *Bargad Ki Beti* (poetry), 1947; *Girti Deewaren,* 1947; *Shehar Mein Ghoomta Aina,* 1962; *Ek Nanhi Kindeel,* 1969; *Bandho Na Nav Is Thanv,* 1974 (all novels); *Toofan Se Pahle* (play); and *Ek Udaseen Sham, Kale Saheb, Jab Santram Ne Balna Uthaya, Kankra Ka Teli, Dachi, Nasoor* and *Ajgar* (all short stories). He was the recipient of Sangeet Natak Akademi Best Playwright Award, 1965 and Soviet Land Nehru Award 1972.

17. USHA MAHAJAN: (1948-   ) She is a journalist and a Hindi short story writer whose works have frequently appeared in *Sarika, Dharamyug, Ravivar, Hans, Navbharat Times* and *Jansatta.* She has translated Khushwant Singh's *Train to Pakistan* into Hindi.

18. YASHPAL: (1903-1976) He was a Hindi novelist with leftist and revolutionary convictions. Among his famous novels are *Dada Comrade, Desh Drohi, Do Duniya, Amita, Jhutha Sach, Chhattis Ghante* and *Phulo Ka Kurta.* He wrote in all about 200 short stories. Important among them are *Sag, Admi Ka Bachcha, Parlok, Pavitrata* and *Kala Admi.*

Umrao Jan Ada
The Courtesan of Lucknow
Mirza Muhammad Hadi Ruswa
Translated by
Khushwant Singh and M A Husaini

This book is an account of Umrao's
life as a Lucknawi courtesan, a nautch girl, told in first
person. The complex characterisation of Umrao, and the life
she lived as a courtesan makes the book memorable and
significant. The book also recreates the culture and decadence
of the aristocratic Lucknawi nawabs.

'An excellent story-teller... Ruswa is one of the best Urdu prose
writers of all times.'

— Khushwant Singh

UNESCO Collection of Representative Works